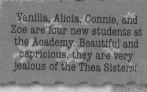
Vanilla, Alicia, Connie, and Zoe are four new students at the Academy. Beautiful and capricious, they are very jealous of the Thea Sisters!

PAULINA'S strong point is courtesy. She really can't stand rude people.

Nicky loves animals and is really in sync with them. She's a member of the environmental group, the "Blue Mice"!

Thea Stilton

PAPERCUTZ™

Thea Stilton

Graphic Novels Available from
PAPERCUTZ

Graphic Novel #1
"The Secret of Whale Island"

Graphic Novel #2
"Revenge of the Lizard Club"

Coming Soon!

THEA STILTON graphic novels are available for $9.99 each only in hardcover. Available from booksellers everywhere. You can also order online from www.papercutz.com or call 1-800-886-1223, Monday through Friday, 9 - 5 EST. MC, Visa, and AmEx accepted. To order by mail, please add $4.00 for postage and handling for first book, add $1.00 for each additional book and make check payable to NBM Publishing. Send to: Papercutz, 40 Exchange Place, Suite 1308, New York, NY 10005.

Thea Stilton

REVENGE OF THE LIZARD CLUB

By Thea Stilton

PAPERCUTZ ™
New York

REVENGE OF THE LIZARD CLUB
© EDIZIONI PIEMME 2008 S.p.A.
Corso Como 15, 20145,
Milan, Italy
Geronimo Stilton and Thea Stilton names, characters and related indicia are copyright,
trademark and exclusive license of Atlantyca S.p.A.
All rights reserved.
The moral right of the author has been asserted.

Text by Thea Stilton
Text Coordination by Lorenza Bernardi and Sarah Rossi (Atlantyca S.p.A.)
Editorial coordination by Patrizia Puricelli and Serena Bellani
Artistic Coordination by Flavio Ferron
With the assistance of Tommaso Valsecchi
Editing by Yellowhale
Editing Coordination and Artwork Supervision by Stefania Bitta and Maryam Funicelli
Script Supervision by Francesco Artibani
Script by Francesco Artibani and Caterina Mognato
Design by Arianna Rea
Art by Raffaella Seccia and Michela Frare
Color by Giulia Basile
With the assistance of Michela Battaglin and Marta Lorini
Cover by Guiseppe Faccioto (design and art) and Daniele Verzini (color)

Based on an original idea by Elisabetta Dami
© 2013 – for this work in English language by Papercutz.
Original title: "La Rivicinta del Club Delle Lucertole"
Translation by: Nanette McGuinness
www.geronimostilton.com

Stilton is the name of a famous English cheese. It is a registered trademark of the
Stilton Cheese Makers' Association. For more information go to www.stiltoncheese.com

Papercutz books may be purchased for business or promotional use. For information on bulk purchases
please contact Macmillan Corporate and Premium Sales Department at (800) 221-7945 x5442.

Lettering and Production -- Big Bird Zatryb
Production Coordinator -- Beth Scorzato
Editor -- Michael Petranek
Jim Salicrup
Editor-in-Chief

ISBN: 978-1-59707-430-8

Printed in China.
July 2013 by WKT Co. LTD.
3/F Phase 1 Leader Industrial Centre
188 Texaco Road, Tsuen Wan, N.T.
Hong Kong

Distributed by Macmillan
First Papercutz Printing

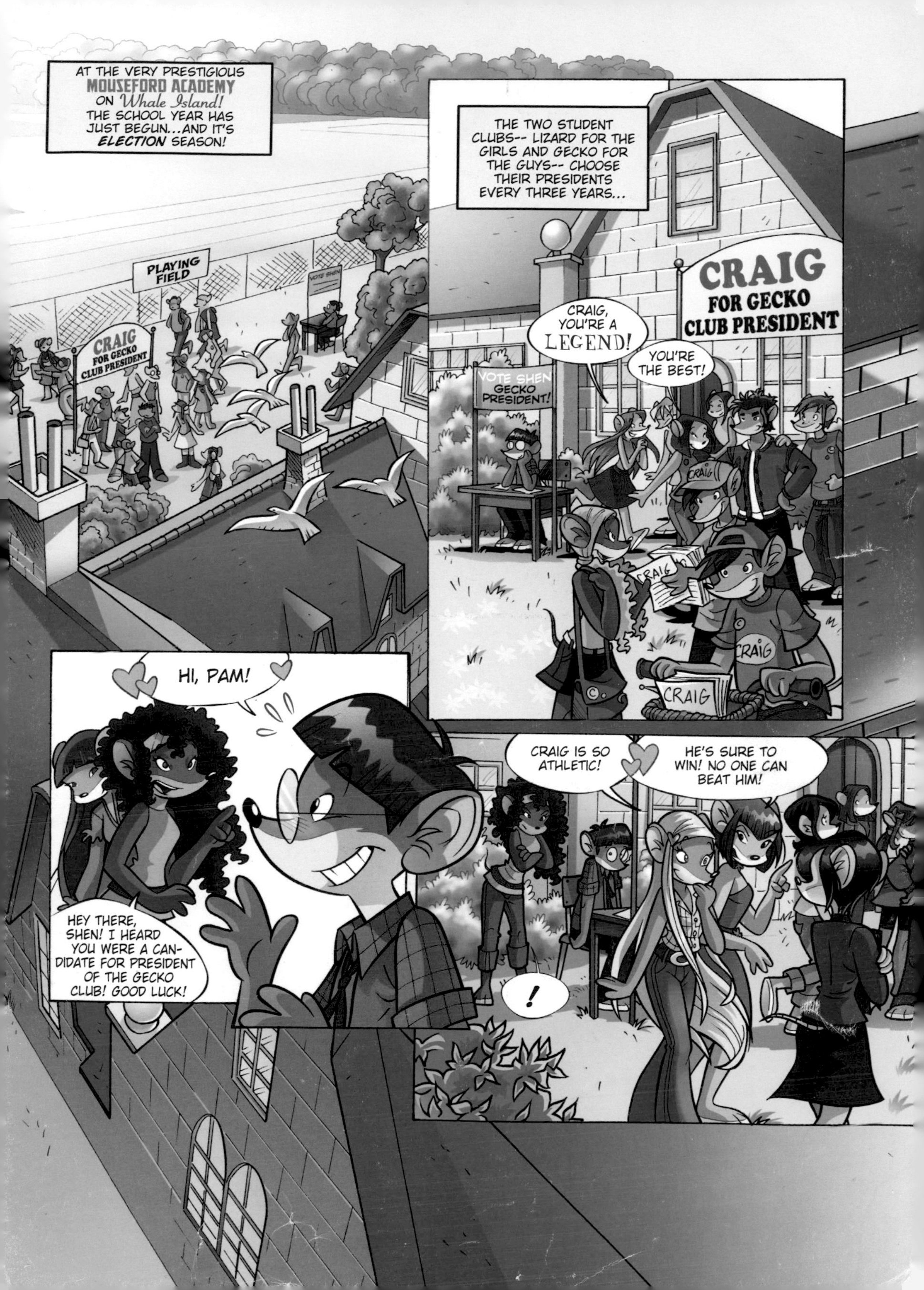
AT THE VERY PRESTIGIOUS MOUSEFORD ACADEMY ON Whale Island! THE SCHOOL YEAR HAS JUST BEGUN...AND IT'S ELECTION SEASON!
PLAYING FIELD
VOTE SHEN
CRAIG FOR GECKO CLUB PRESIDENT
THE TWO STUDENT CLUBS-- LIZARD FOR THE GIRLS AND GECKO FOR THE GUYS-- CHOOSE THEIR PRESIDENTS EVERY THREE YEARS...
CRAIG FOR GECKO CLUB PRESIDENT
CRAIG, YOU'RE A LEGEND!
YOU'RE THE BEST!
VOTE SHEN GECKO PRESIDENT!
CRAIG
CRAIG
CRAIG
CRAIG
HI, PAM!
HEY THERE, SHEN! I HEARD YOU WERE A CANDIDATE FOR PRESIDENT OF THE GECKO CLUB! GOOD LUCK!
CRAIG IS SO ATHLETIC!
HE'S SURE TO WIN! NO ONE CAN BEAT HIM!
!

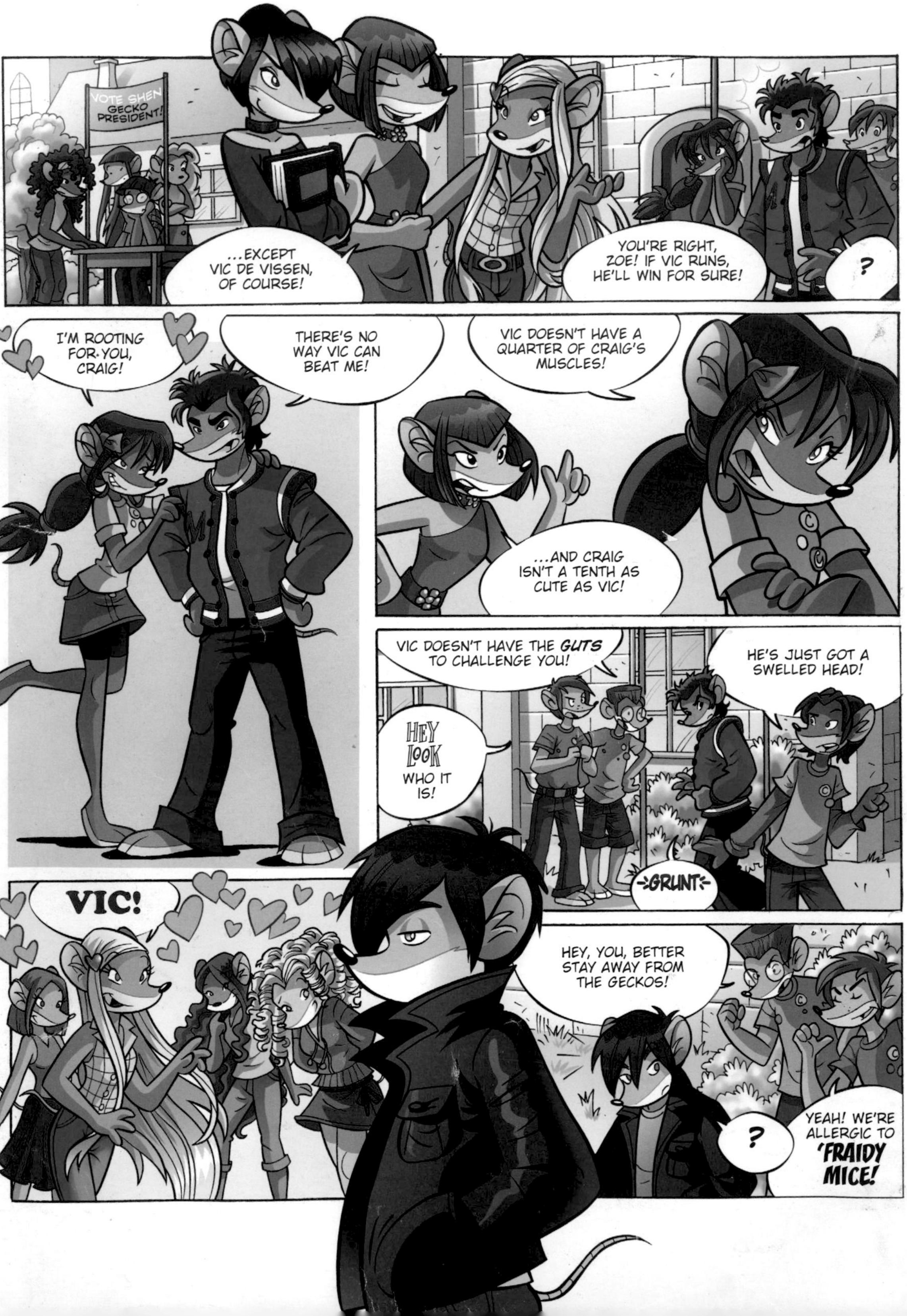
VOTE SHEN GECKO PRESIDENT!
...EXCEPT VIC DE VISSEN, OF COURSE!
YOU'RE RIGHT, ZOE! IF VIC RUNS, HE'LL WIN FOR SURE!
?
I'M ROOTING FOR YOU, CRAIG!
THERE'S NO WAY VIC CAN BEAT ME!
VIC DOESN'T HAVE A QUARTER OF CRAIG'S MUSCLES!
...AND CRAIG ISN'T A TENTH AS CUTE AS VIC!
VIC DOESN'T HAVE THE GUTS TO CHALLENGE YOU!
HE'S JUST GOT A SWELLED HEAD!
HEY LOOK WHO IT IS!
GRUNT
VIC!
HEY, YOU, BETTER STAY AWAY FROM THE GECKOS!
?
YEAH! WE'RE ALLERGIC TO 'FRAIDY MICE!

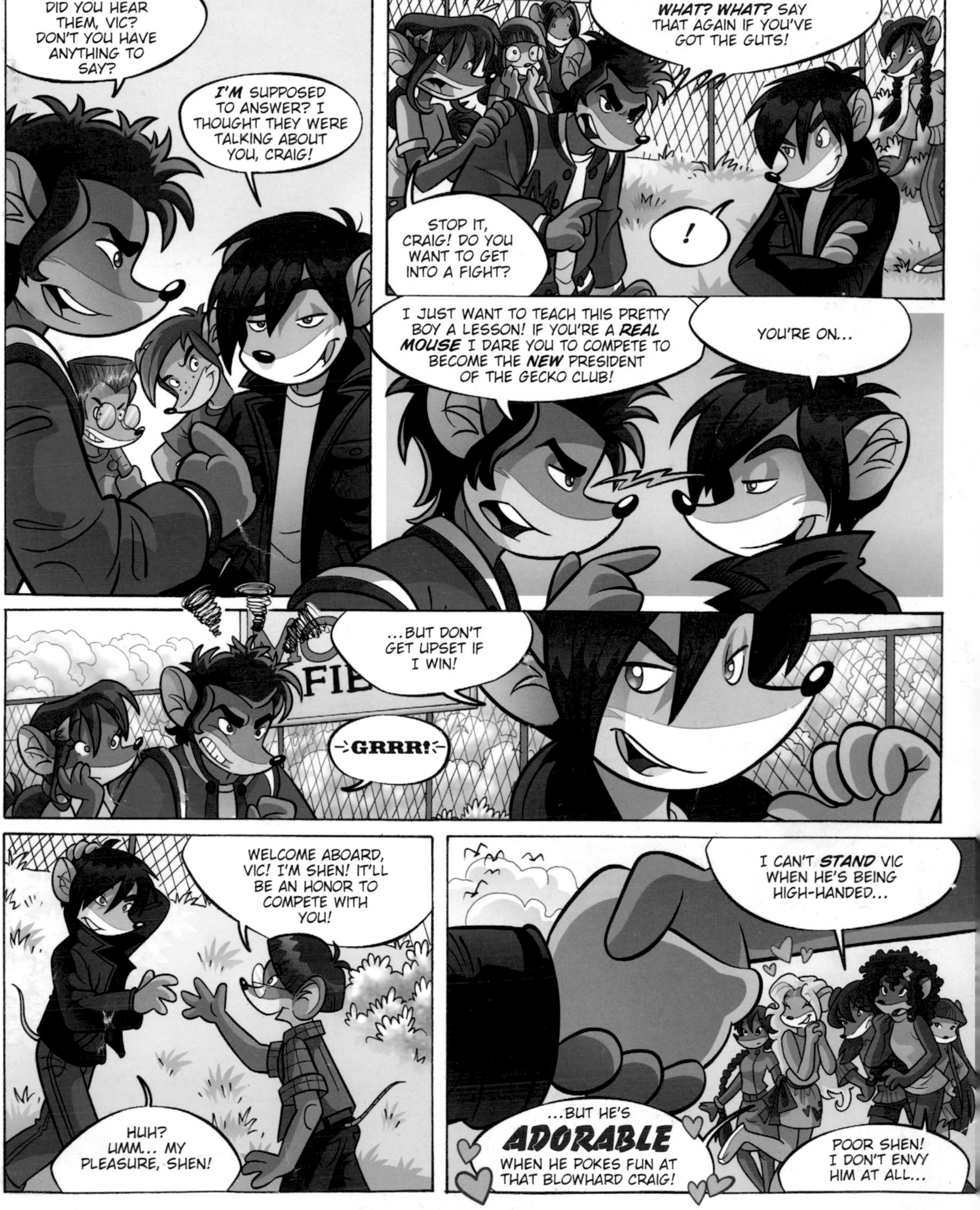
DID YOU HEAR THEM, VIC? DON'T YOU HAVE ANYTHING TO SAY?
I'M SUPPOSED TO ANSWER? I THOUGHT THEY WERE TALKING ABOUT YOU, CRAIG!
WHAT? WHAT? SAY THAT AGAIN IF YOU'VE GOT THE GUTS!
STOP IT, CRAIG! DO YOU WANT TO GET INTO A FIGHT?
!
I JUST WANT TO TEACH THIS PRETTY BOY A LESSON! IF YOU'RE A REAL MOUSE I DARE YOU TO COMPETE TO BECOME THE NEW PRESIDENT OF THE GECKO CLUB!
YOU'RE ON...
...BUT DON'T GET UPSET IF I WIN!
GRRR!
WELCOME ABOARD, VIC! I'M SHEN! IT'LL BE AN HONOR TO COMPETE WITH YOU!
HUH? UMM... MY PLEASURE, SHEN!
I CAN'T STAND VIC WHEN HE'S BEING HIGH-HANDED...
...BUT HE'S ADORABLE WHEN HE POKES FUN AT THAT BLOWHARD CRAIG!
POOR SHEN! I DON'T ENVY HIM AT ALL...

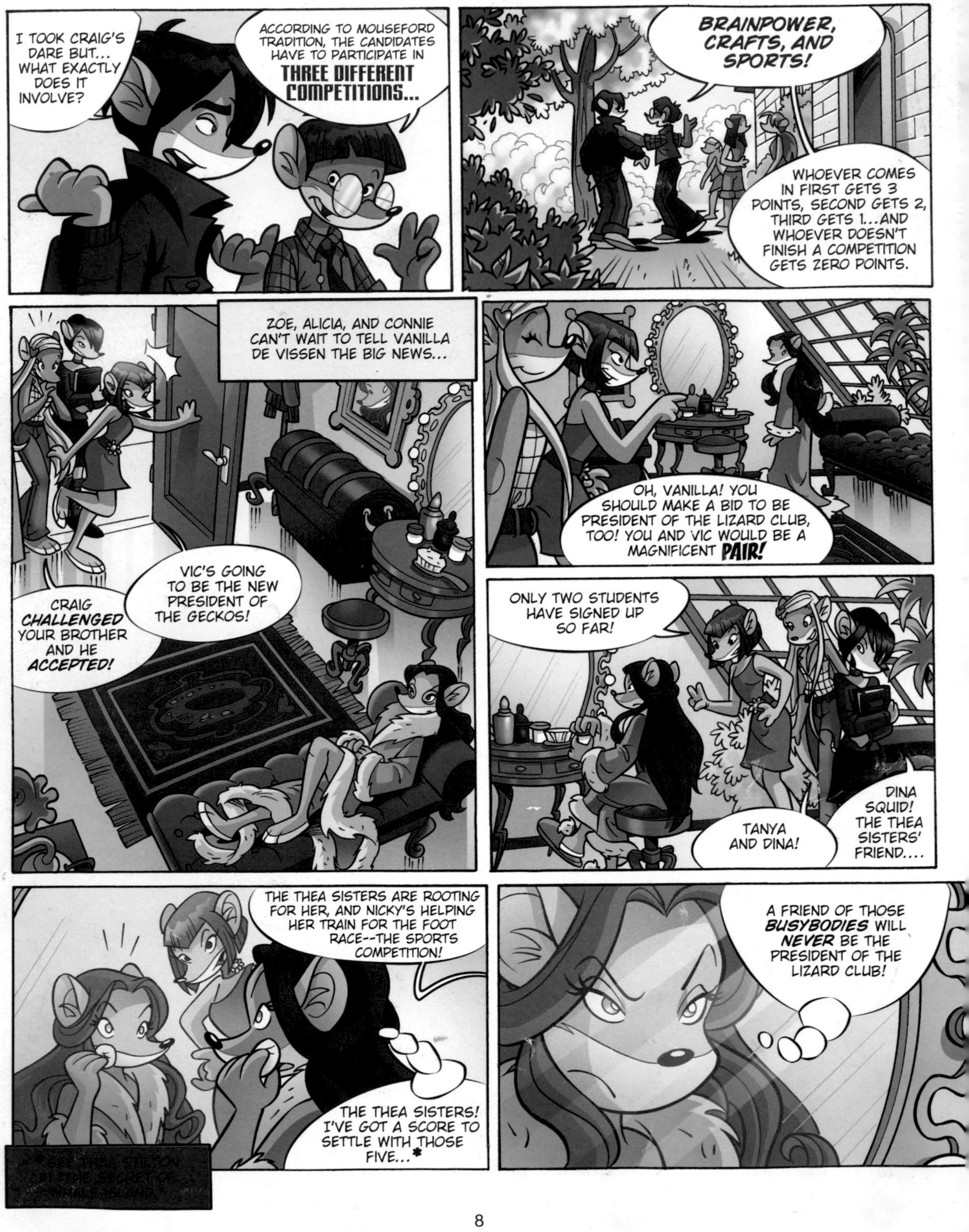
I TOOK CRAIG'S DARE BUT... WHAT EXACTLY DOES IT INVOLVE?
ACCORDING TO MOUSEFORD TRADITION, THE CANDIDATES HAVE TO PARTICIPATE IN THREE DIFFERENT COMPETITIONS...
BRAINPOWER, CRAFTS, AND SPORTS!
WHOEVER COMES IN FIRST GETS 3 POINTS, SECOND GETS 2, THIRD GETS 1...AND WHOEVER DOESN'T FINISH A COMPETITION GETS ZERO POINTS.
ZOE, ALICIA, AND CONNIE CAN'T WAIT TO TELL VANILLA DE VISSEN THE BIG NEWS...
CRAIG CHALLENGED YOUR BROTHER AND HE ACCEPTED!
VIC'S GOING TO BE THE NEW PRESIDENT OF THE GECKOS!
OH, VANILLA! YOU SHOULD MAKE A BID TO BE PRESIDENT OF THE LIZARD CLUB, TOO! YOU AND VIC WOULD BE A MAGNIFICENT PAIR!
ONLY TWO STUDENTS HAVE SIGNED UP SO FAR!
TANYA AND DINA!
DINA SQUID! THE THEA SISTERS' FRIEND....
THE THEA SISTERS ARE ROOTING FOR HER, AND NICKY'S HELPING HER TRAIN FOR THE FOOT RACE--THE SPORTS COMPETITION!
THE THEA SISTERS! I'VE GOT A SCORE TO SETTLE WITH THOSE FIVE...*
[redacted]
A FRIEND OF THOSE BUSYBODIES WILL NEVER BE THE PRESIDENT OF THE LIZARD CLUB!

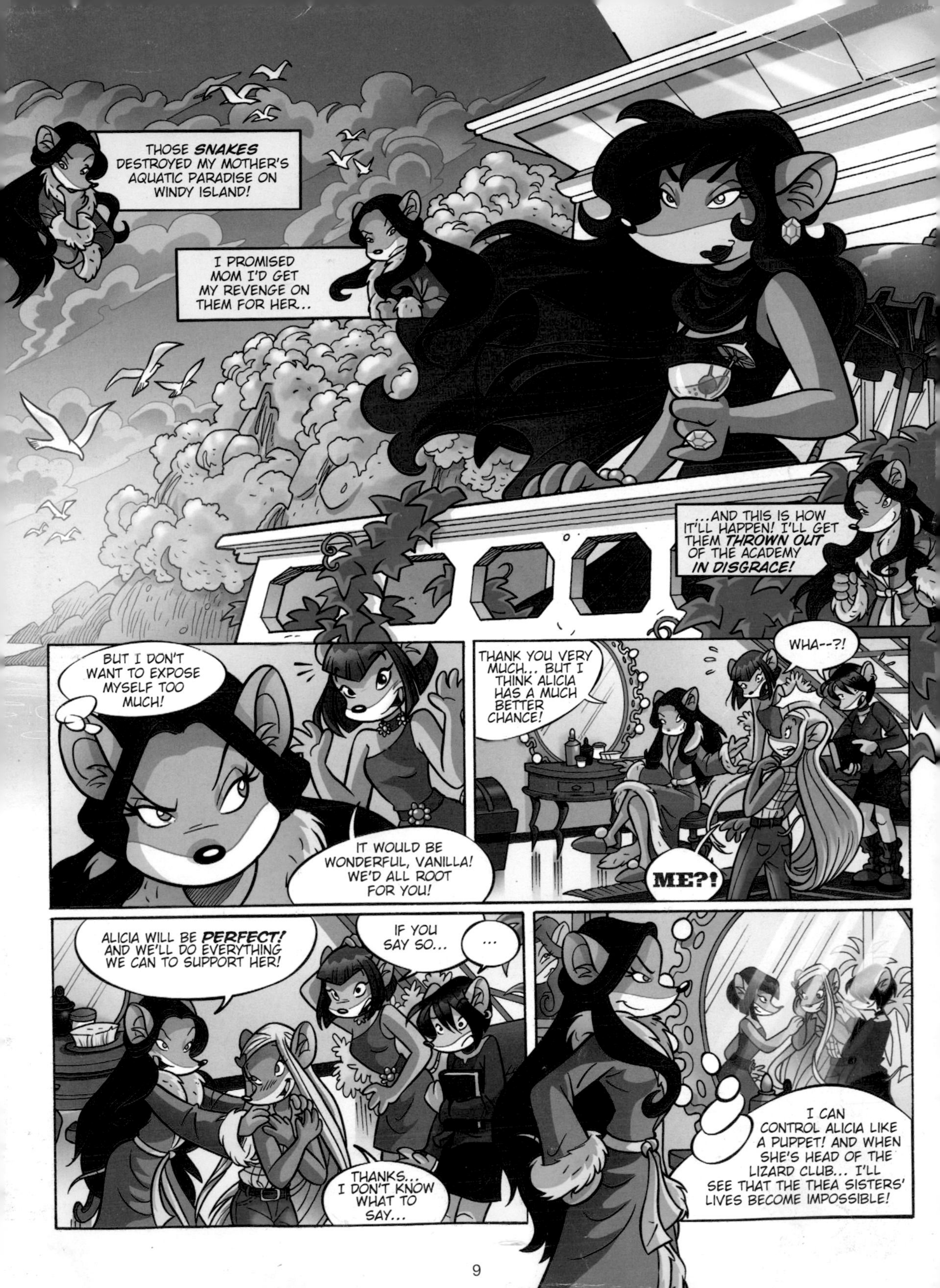

THOSE SNAKES DESTROYED MY MOTHER'S AQUATIC PARADISE ON WINDY ISLAND!
I PROMISED MOM I'D GET MY REVENGE ON THEM FOR HER...
...AND THIS IS HOW IT'LL HAPPEN! I'LL GET THEM THROWN OUT OF THE ACADEMY IN DISGRACE!
BUT I DON'T WANT TO EXPOSE MYSELF TOO MUCH!
IT WOULD BE WONDERFUL, VANILLA! WE'D ALL ROOT FOR YOU!
THANK YOU VERY MUCH... BUT I THINK ALICIA HAS A MUCH BETTER CHANCE!
WHA--?!
ME?!
ALICIA WILL BE PERFECT! AND WE'LL DO EVERYTHING WE CAN TO SUPPORT HER!
IF YOU SAY SO...
...
THANKS... I DON'T KNOW WHAT TO SAY...
I CAN CONTROL ALICIA LIKE A PUPPET! AND WHEN SHE'S HEAD OF THE LIZARD CLUB... I'LL SEE THAT THE THEA SISTERS' LIVES BECOME IMPOSSIBLE!

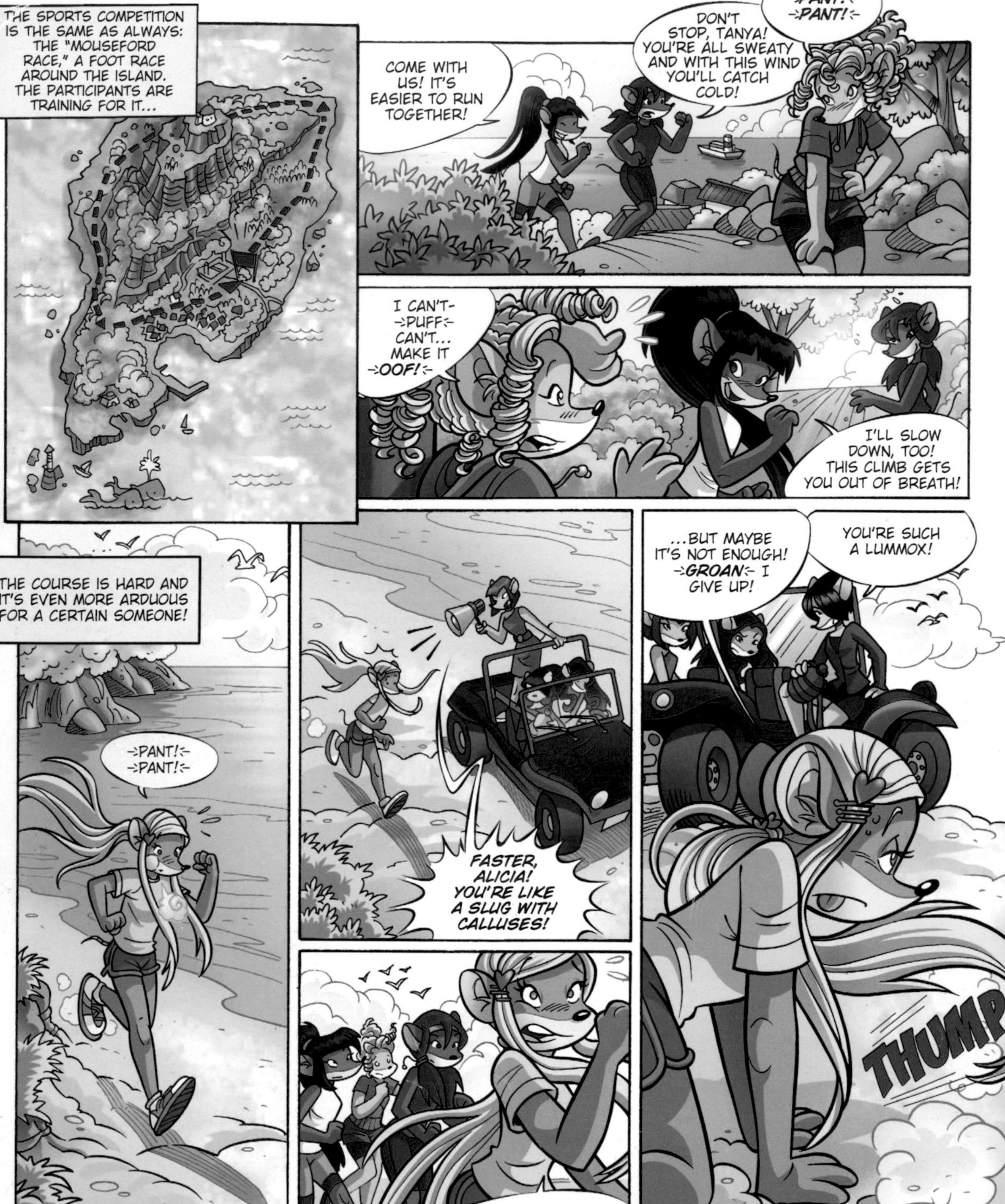
THE SPORTS COMPETITION IS THE SAME AS ALWAYS: THE "MOUSEFORD RACE," A FOOT RACE AROUND THE ISLAND. THE PARTICIPANTS ARE TRAINING FOR IT...
COME WITH US! IT'S EASIER TO RUN TOGETHER!
DON'T STOP, TANYA! YOU'RE ALL SWEATY AND WITH THIS WIND YOU'LL CATCH COLD!
-PANT!- -PANT!-
I CAN'T- -PUFF- CAN'T... MAKE IT -OOF!-
I'LL SLOW DOWN, TOO! THIS CLIMB GETS YOU OUT OF BREATH!
THE COURSE IS HARD AND IT'S EVEN MORE ARDUOUS FOR A CERTAIN SOMEONE!
-PANT!- -PANT!-
FASTER, ALICIA! YOU'RE LIKE A SLUG WITH CALLUSES!
-HUFF- I'M GIVING IT EVERYTHING I'VE GOT...
...BUT MAYBE IT'S NOT ENOUGH! -GROAN- I GIVE UP!
YOU'RE SUCH A LUMMOX!
THUMP

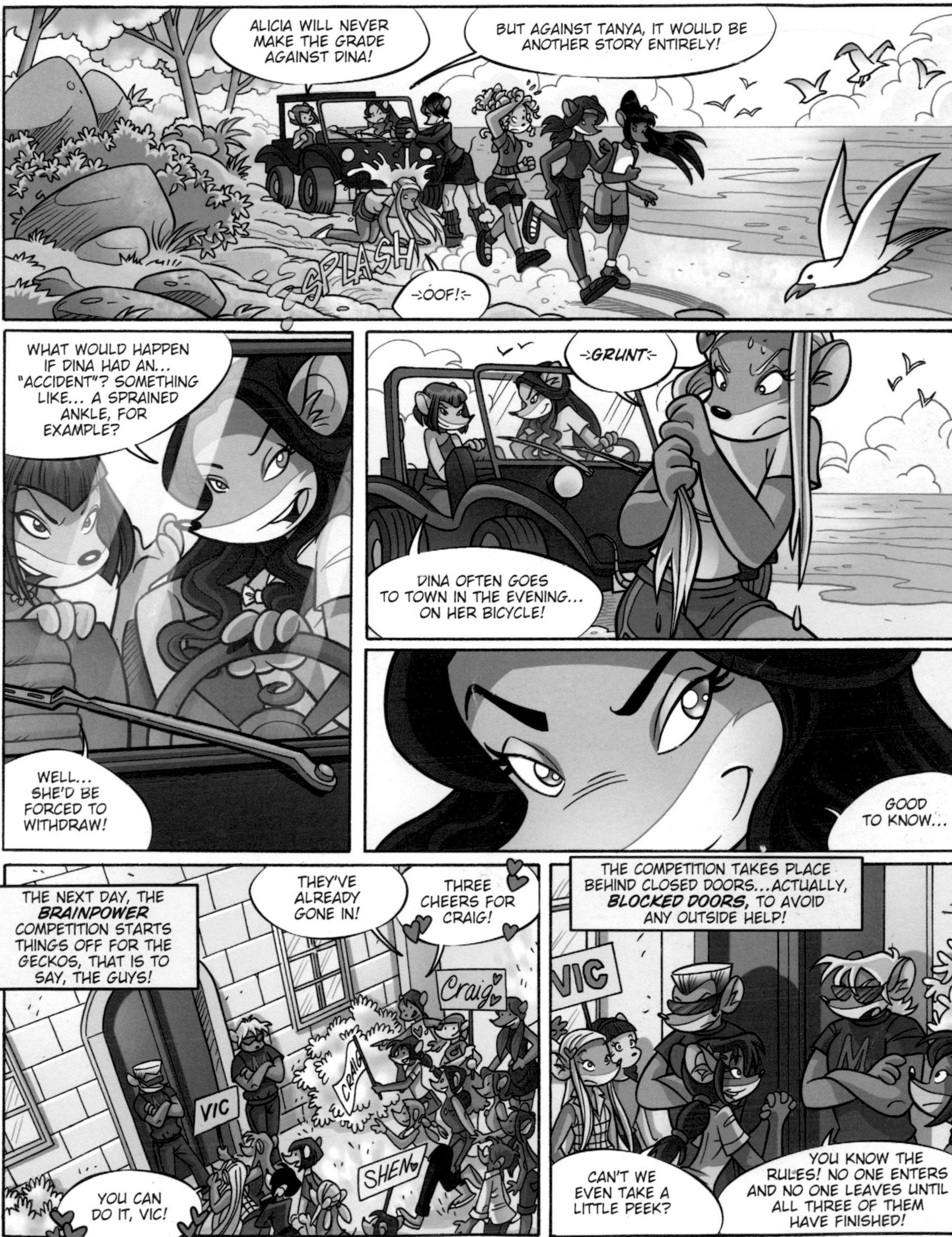
ALICIA WILL NEVER MAKE THE GRADE AGAINST DINA!
BUT AGAINST TANYA, IT WOULD BE ANOTHER STORY ENTIRELY!
SPLASH!
OOF!
WHAT WOULD HAPPEN IF DINA HAD AN... "ACCIDENT"? SOMETHING LIKE... A SPRAINED ANKLE, FOR EXAMPLE?
WELL... SHE'D BE FORCED TO WITHDRAW!
GRUNT
DINA OFTEN GOES TO TOWN IN THE EVENING... ON HER BICYCLE!
GOOD TO KNOW...
THE NEXT DAY, THE BRAINPOWER COMPETITION STARTS THINGS OFF FOR THE GECKOS, THAT IS TO SAY, THE GUYS!
THEY'VE ALREADY GONE IN!
THREE CHEERS FOR CRAIG!
Craig
CRAIG
VIC
SHEN
YOU CAN DO IT, VIC!
THE COMPETITION TAKES PLACE BEHIND CLOSED DOORS...ACTUALLY, BLOCKED DOORS, TO AVOID ANY OUTSIDE HELP!
VIC
CAN'T WE EVEN TAKE A LITTLE PEEK?
YOU KNOW THE RULES! NO ONE ENTERS AND NO ONE LEAVES UNTIL ALL THREE OF THEM HAVE FINISHED!

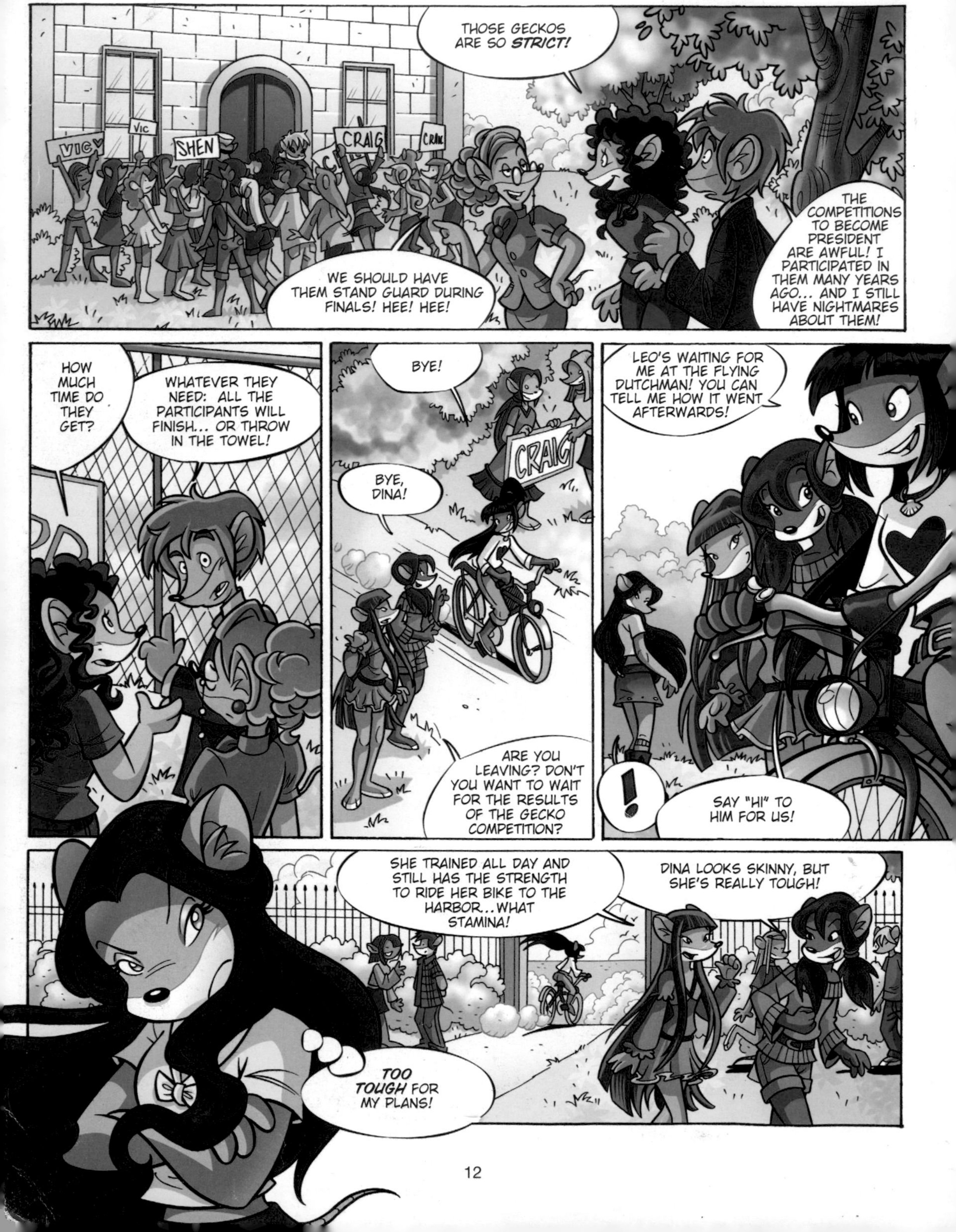
THOSE GECKOS ARE SO STRICT!
VIC
VIC
SHEN
CRAIG
CRAIG
WE SHOULD HAVE THEM STAND GUARD DURING FINALS! HEE! HEE!
THE COMPETITIONS TO BECOME PRESIDENT ARE AWFUL! I PARTICIPATED IN THEM MANY YEARS AGO... AND I STILL HAVE NIGHTMARES ABOUT THEM!
HOW MUCH TIME DO THEY GET?
WHATEVER THEY NEED: ALL THE PARTICIPANTS WILL FINISH... OR THROW IN THE TOWEL!
BYE!
CRAIG
BYE, DINA!
ARE YOU LEAVING? DON'T YOU WANT TO WAIT FOR THE RESULTS OF THE GECKO COMPETITION?
LEO'S WAITING FOR ME AT THE FLYING DUTCHMAN! YOU CAN TELL ME HOW IT WENT AFTERWARDS!
!
SAY "HI" TO HIM FOR US!
SHE TRAINED ALL DAY AND STILL HAS THE STRENGTH TO RIDE HER BIKE TO THE HARBOR...WHAT STAMINA!
DINA LOOKS SKINNY, BUT SHE'S REALLY TOUGH!
TOO TOUGH FOR MY PLANS!

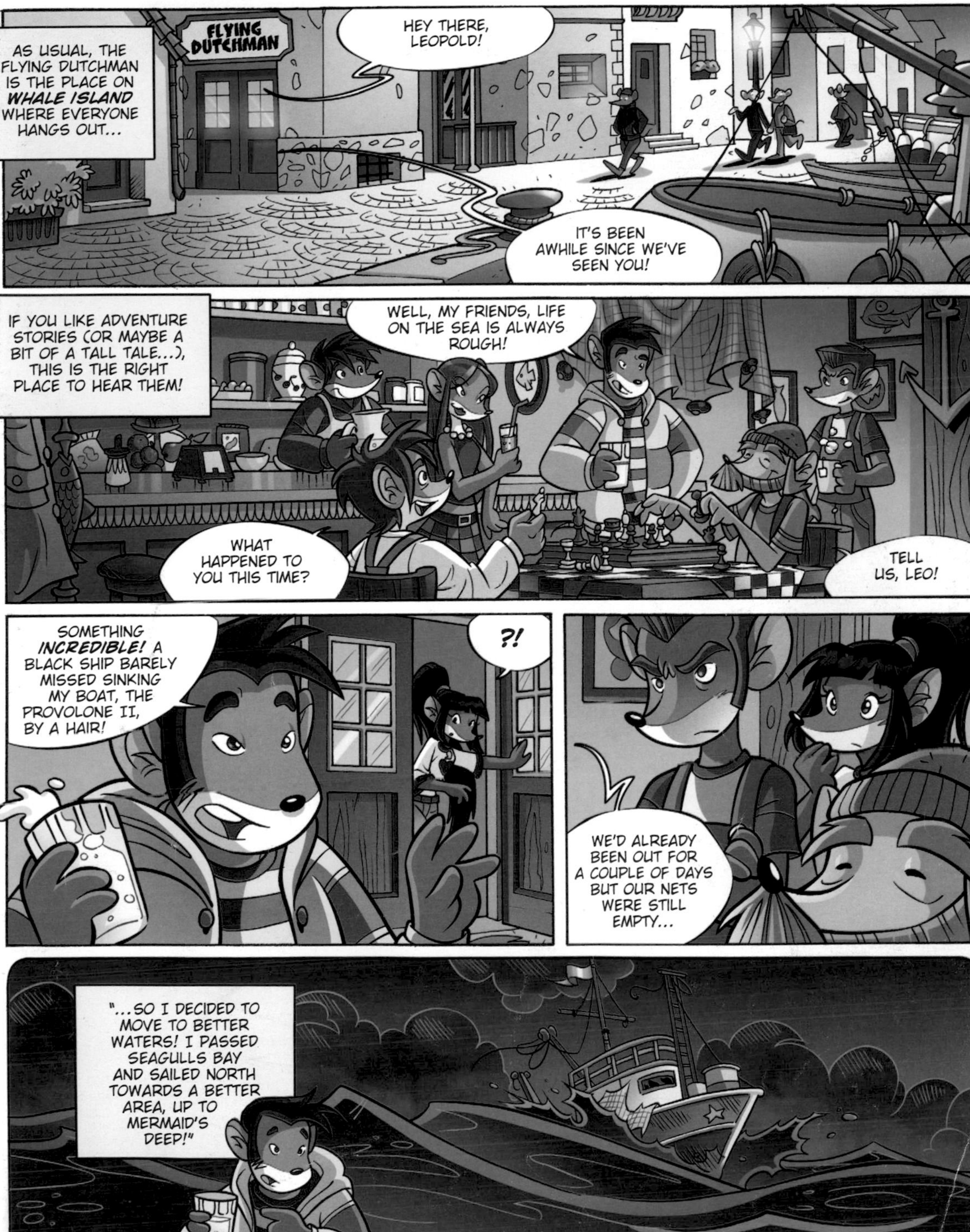
FLYING DUTCHMAN
AS USUAL, THE FLYING DUTCHMAN IS THE PLACE ON *WHALE ISLAND* WHERE EVERYONE HANGS OUT...
HEY THERE, LEOPOLD!
IT'S BEEN AWHILE SINCE WE'VE SEEN YOU!
IF YOU LIKE ADVENTURE STORIES (OR MAYBE A BIT OF A TALL TALE...), THIS IS THE RIGHT PLACE TO HEAR THEM!
WELL, MY FRIENDS, LIFE ON THE SEA IS ALWAYS ROUGH!
WHAT HAPPENED TO YOU THIS TIME?
TELL US, LEO!
SOMETHING *INCREDIBLE!* A BLACK SHIP BARELY MISSED SINKING MY BOAT, THE PROVOLONE II, BY A HAIR!
?!
WE'D ALREADY BEEN OUT FOR A COUPLE OF DAYS BUT OUR NETS WERE STILL EMPTY...
"...SO I DECIDED TO MOVE TO BETTER WATERS! I PASSED SEAGULLS BAY AND SAILED NORTH TOWARDS A BETTER AREA, UP TO MERMAID'S DEEP!"

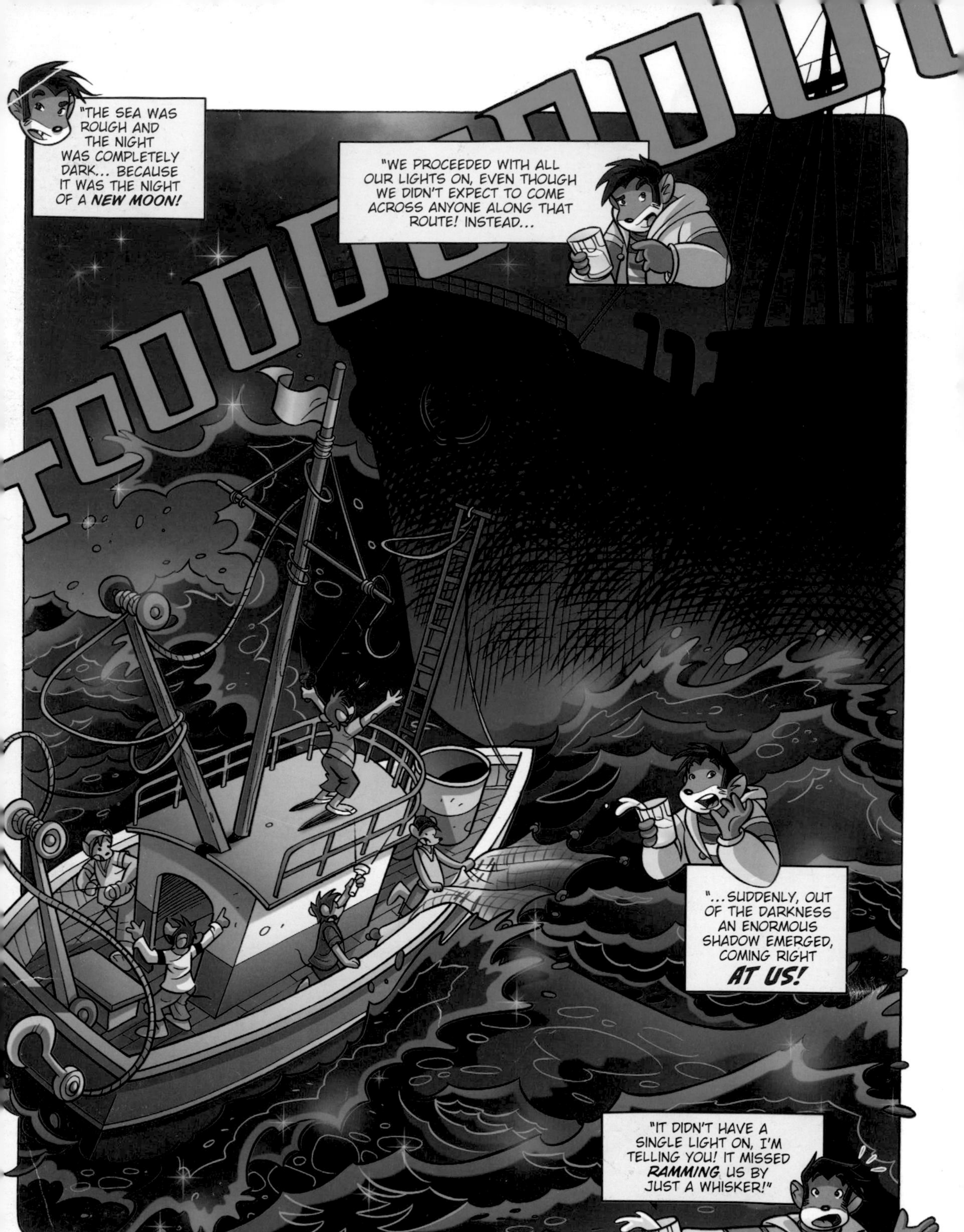
"THE SEA WAS ROUGH AND THE NIGHT WAS COMPLETELY DARK... BECAUSE IT WAS THE NIGHT OF A NEW MOON!
"WE PROCEEDED WITH ALL OUR LIGHTS ON, EVEN THOUGH WE DIDN'T EXPECT TO COME ACROSS ANYONE ALONG THAT ROUTE! INSTEAD...
"...SUDDENLY, OUT OF THE DARKNESS AN ENORMOUS SHADOW EMERGED, COMING RIGHT AT US!
"IT DIDN'T HAVE A SINGLE LIGHT ON, I'M TELLING YOU! IT MISSED RAMMING US BY JUST A WHISKER!"

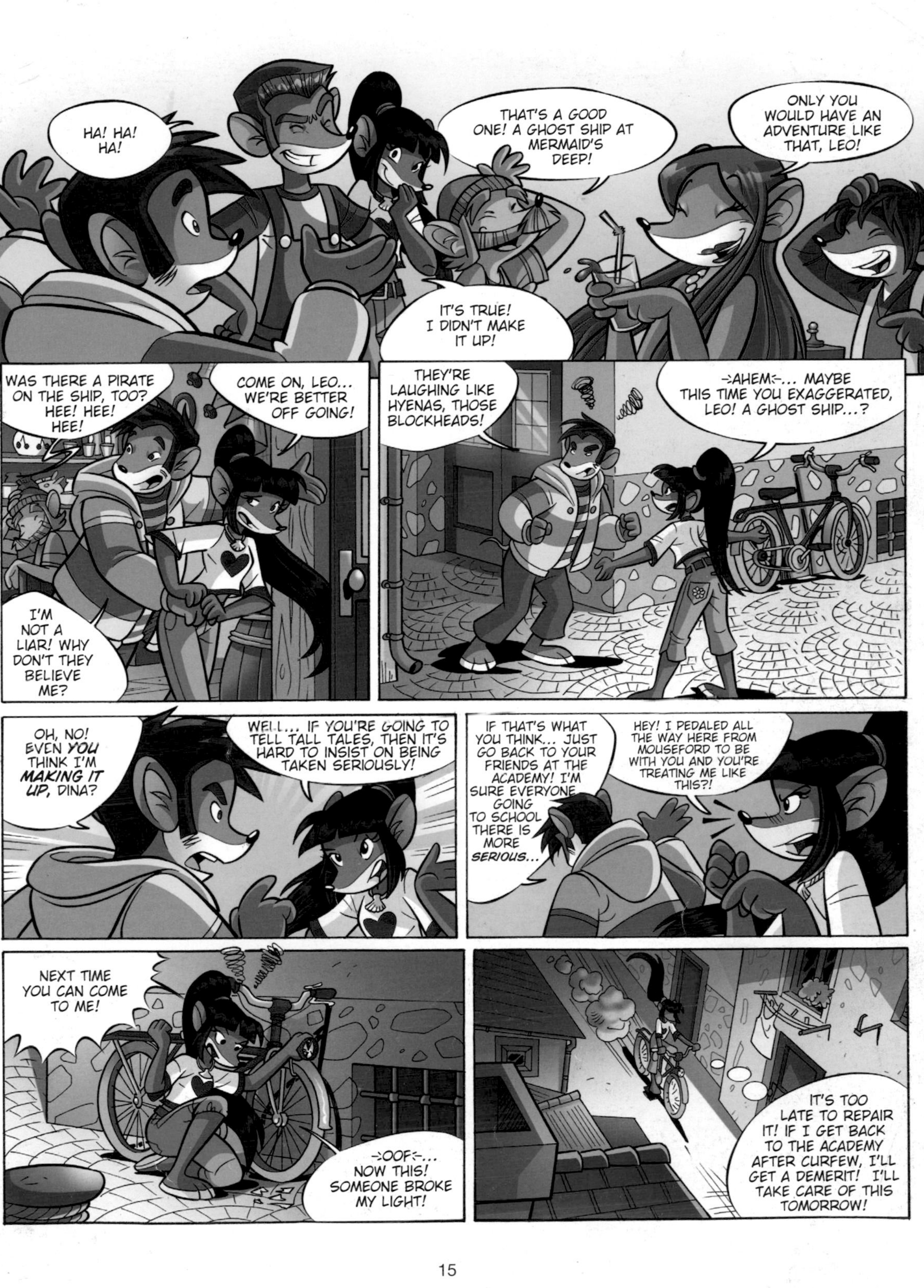
HA! HA! HA!
THAT'S A GOOD ONE! A GHOST SHIP AT MERMAID'S DEEP!
ONLY YOU WOULD HAVE AN ADVENTURE LIKE THAT, LEO!
IT'S TRUE! I DIDN'T MAKE IT UP!
WAS THERE A PIRATE ON THE SHIP, TOO? HEE! HEE! HEE!
COME ON, LEO... WE'RE BETTER OFF GOING!
I'M NOT A LIAR! WHY DON'T THEY BELIEVE ME?
THEY'RE LAUGHING LIKE HYENAS, THOSE BLOCKHEADS!
-AHEM-... MAYBE THIS TIME YOU EXAGGERATED, LEO! A GHOST SHIP...?
OH, NO! EVEN YOU THINK I'M MAKING IT UP, DINA?
WELL... IF YOU'RE GOING TO TELL TALL TALES, THEN IT'S HARD TO INSIST ON BEING TAKEN SERIOUSLY!
IF THAT'S WHAT YOU THINK... JUST GO BACK TO YOUR FRIENDS AT THE ACADEMY! I'M SURE EVERYONE GOING TO SCHOOL THERE IS MORE SERIOUS...
HEY! I PEDALED ALL THE WAY HERE FROM MOUSEFORD TO BE WITH YOU AND YOU'RE TREATING ME LIKE THIS?!
NEXT TIME YOU CAN COME TO ME!
-OOF-... NOW THIS! SOMEONE BROKE MY LIGHT!
IT'S TOO LATE TO REPAIR IT! IF I GET BACK TO THE ACADEMY AFTER CURFEW, I'LL GET A DEMERIT! I'LL TAKE CARE OF THIS TOMORROW!

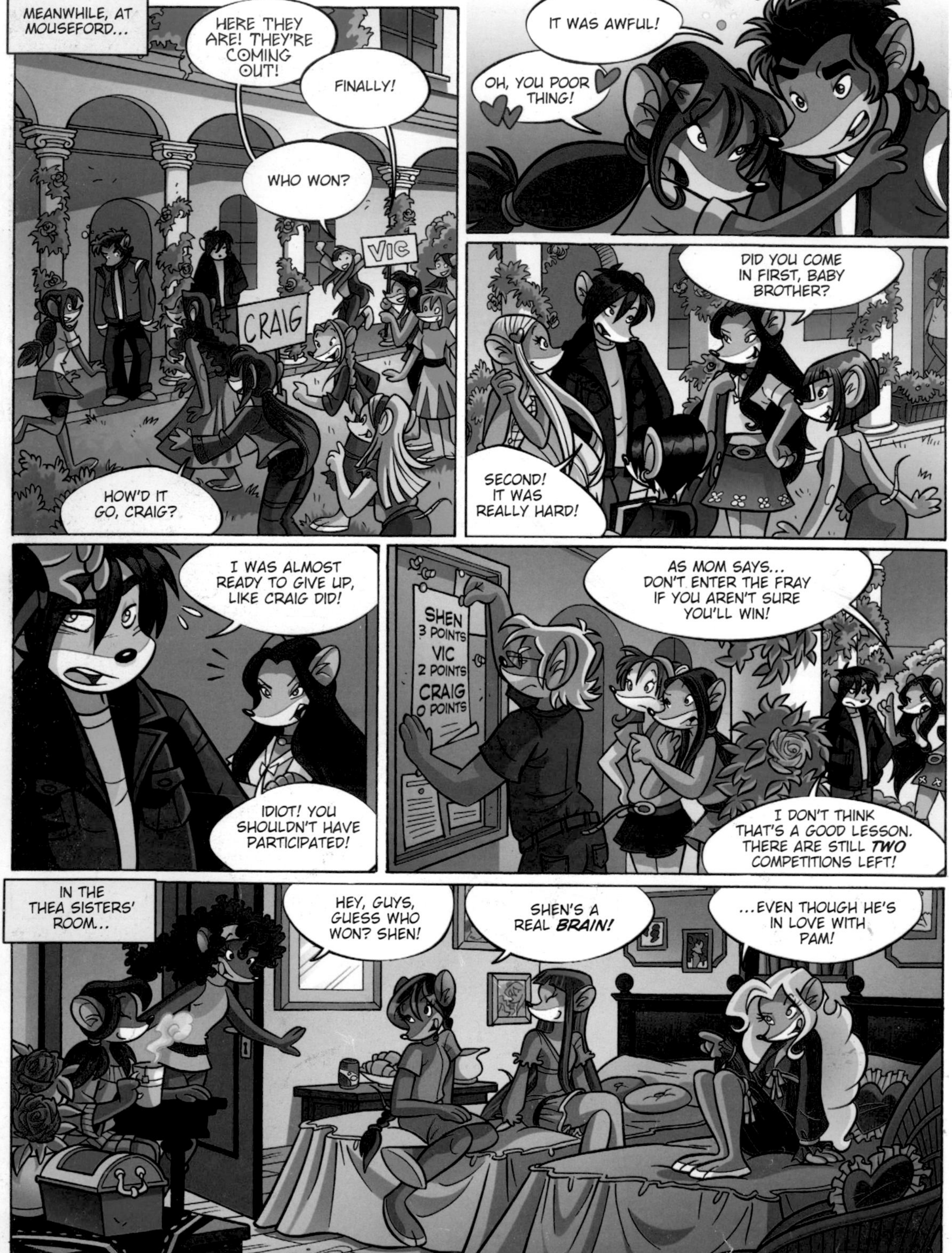
MEANWHILE, AT MOUSEFORD...
HERE THEY ARE! THEY'RE COMING OUT!
FINALLY!
WHO WON?
VIC
CRAIG
HOW'D IT GO, CRAIG?
IT WAS AWFUL!
OH, YOU POOR THING!
DID YOU COME IN FIRST, BABY BROTHER?
SECOND! IT WAS REALLY HARD!
I WAS ALMOST READY TO GIVE UP, LIKE CRAIG DID!
IDIOT! YOU SHOULDN'T HAVE PARTICIPATED!
SHEN 3 POINTS
VIC 2 POINTS
CRAIG 0 POINTS
AS MOM SAYS... DON'T ENTER THE FRAY IF YOU AREN'T SURE YOU'LL WIN!
I DON'T THINK THAT'S A GOOD LESSON. THERE ARE STILL TWO COMPETITIONS LEFT!
IN THE THEA SISTERS' ROOM...
HEY, GUYS, GUESS WHO WON? SHEN!
SHEN'S A REAL BRAIN!
...EVEN THOUGH HE'S IN LOVE WITH PAM!

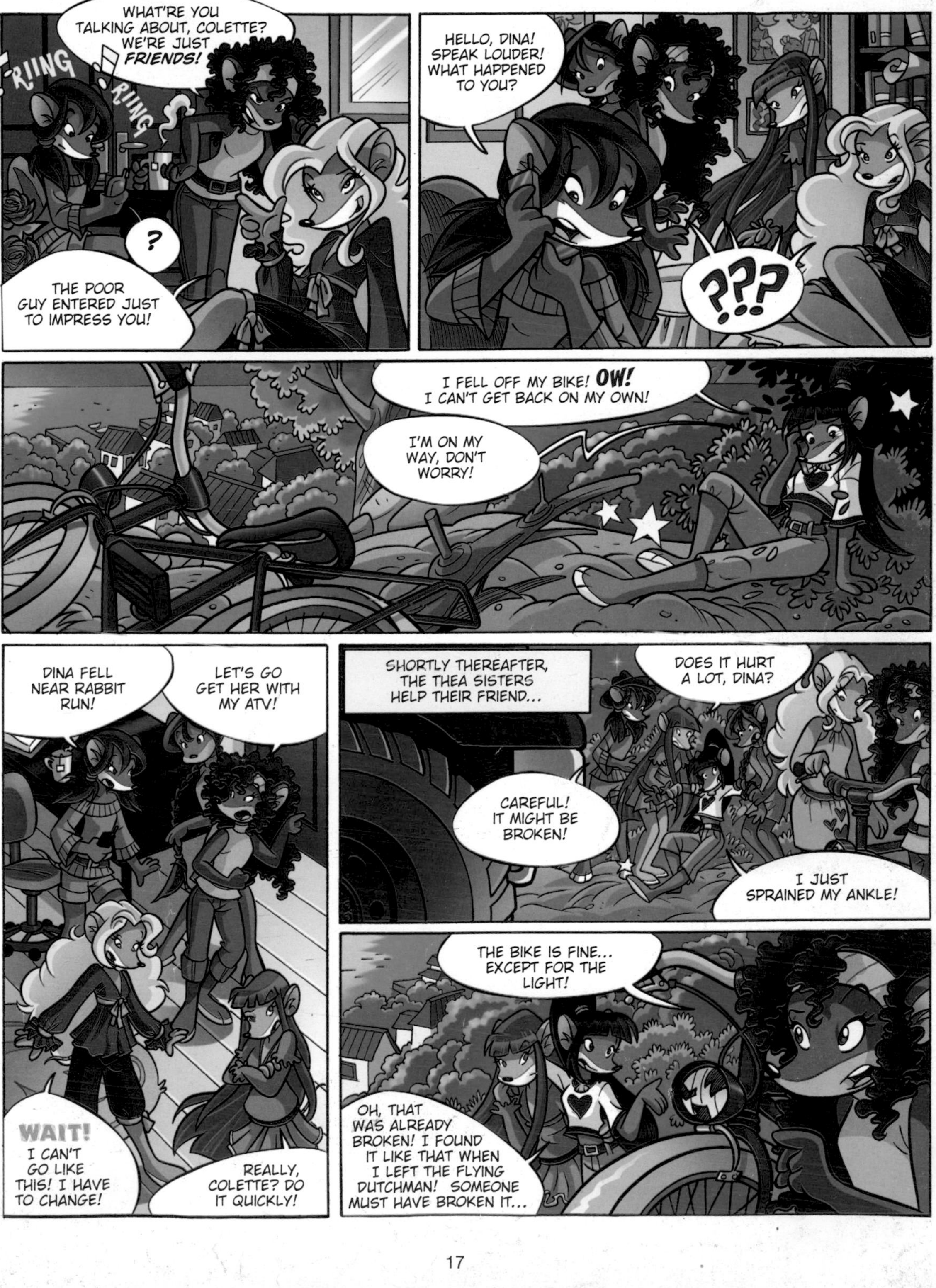
RIING
RIING
WHAT'RE YOU TALKING ABOUT, COLETTE? WE'RE JUST FRIENDS!
?
THE POOR GUY ENTERED JUST TO IMPRESS YOU!
HELLO, DINA! SPEAK LOUDER! WHAT HAPPENED TO YOU?
???
I FELL OFF MY BIKE! OW! I CAN'T GET BACK ON MY OWN!
I'M ON MY WAY, DON'T WORRY!
DINA FELL NEAR RABBIT RUN!
LET'S GO GET HER WITH MY ATV!
WAIT! I CAN'T GO LIKE THIS! I HAVE TO CHANGE!
REALLY, COLETTE? DO IT QUICKLY!
SHORTLY THEREAFTER, THE THEA SISTERS HELP THEIR FRIEND...
DOES IT HURT A LOT, DINA?
CAREFUL! IT MIGHT BE BROKEN!
I JUST SPRAINED MY ANKLE!
THE BIKE IS FINE... EXCEPT FOR THE LIGHT!
OH, THAT WAS ALREADY BROKEN! I FOUND IT LIKE THAT WHEN I LEFT THE FLYING DUTCHMAN! SOMEONE MUST HAVE BROKEN IT...

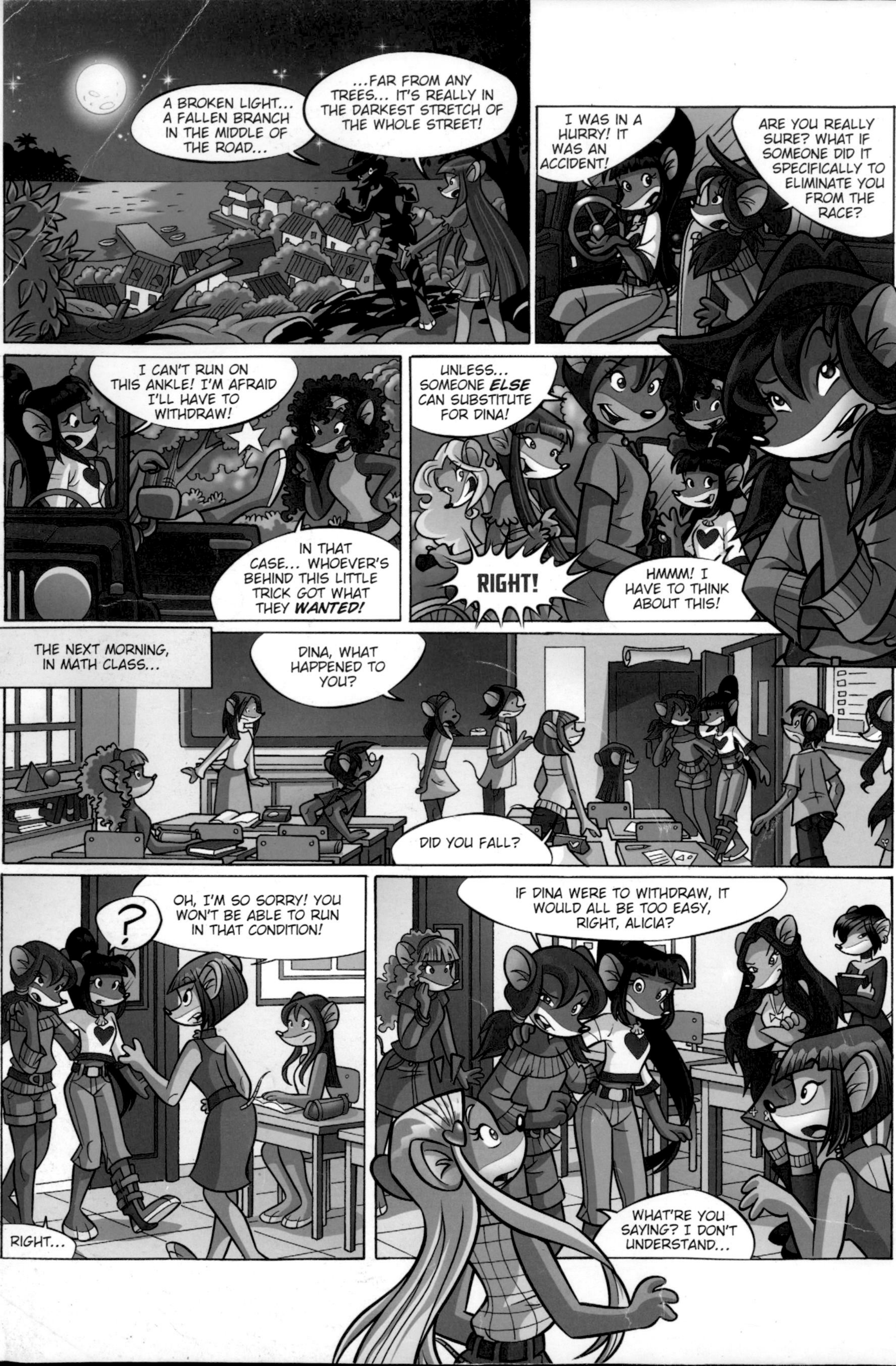
A BROKEN LIGHT... A FALLEN BRANCH IN THE MIDDLE OF THE ROAD...
...FAR FROM ANY TREES... IT'S REALLY IN THE DARKEST STRETCH OF THE WHOLE STREET!
I WAS IN A HURRY! IT WAS AN ACCIDENT!
ARE YOU REALLY SURE? WHAT IF SOMEONE DID IT SPECIFICALLY TO ELIMINATE YOU FROM THE RACE?
I CAN'T RUN ON THIS ANKLE! I'M AFRAID I'LL HAVE TO WITHDRAW!
IN THAT CASE... WHOEVER'S BEHIND THIS LITTLE TRICK GOT WHAT THEY WANTED!
UNLESS... SOMEONE ELSE CAN SUBSTITUTE FOR DINA!
RIGHT!
HMMM! I HAVE TO THINK ABOUT THIS!
THE NEXT MORNING, IN MATH CLASS...
DINA, WHAT HAPPENED TO YOU?
DID YOU FALL?
?
OH, I'M SO SORRY! YOU WON'T BE ABLE TO RUN IN THAT CONDITION!
RIGHT...
IF DINA WERE TO WITHDRAW, IT WOULD ALL BE TOO EASY, RIGHT, ALICIA?
WHAT'RE YOU SAYING? I DON'T UNDERSTAND...

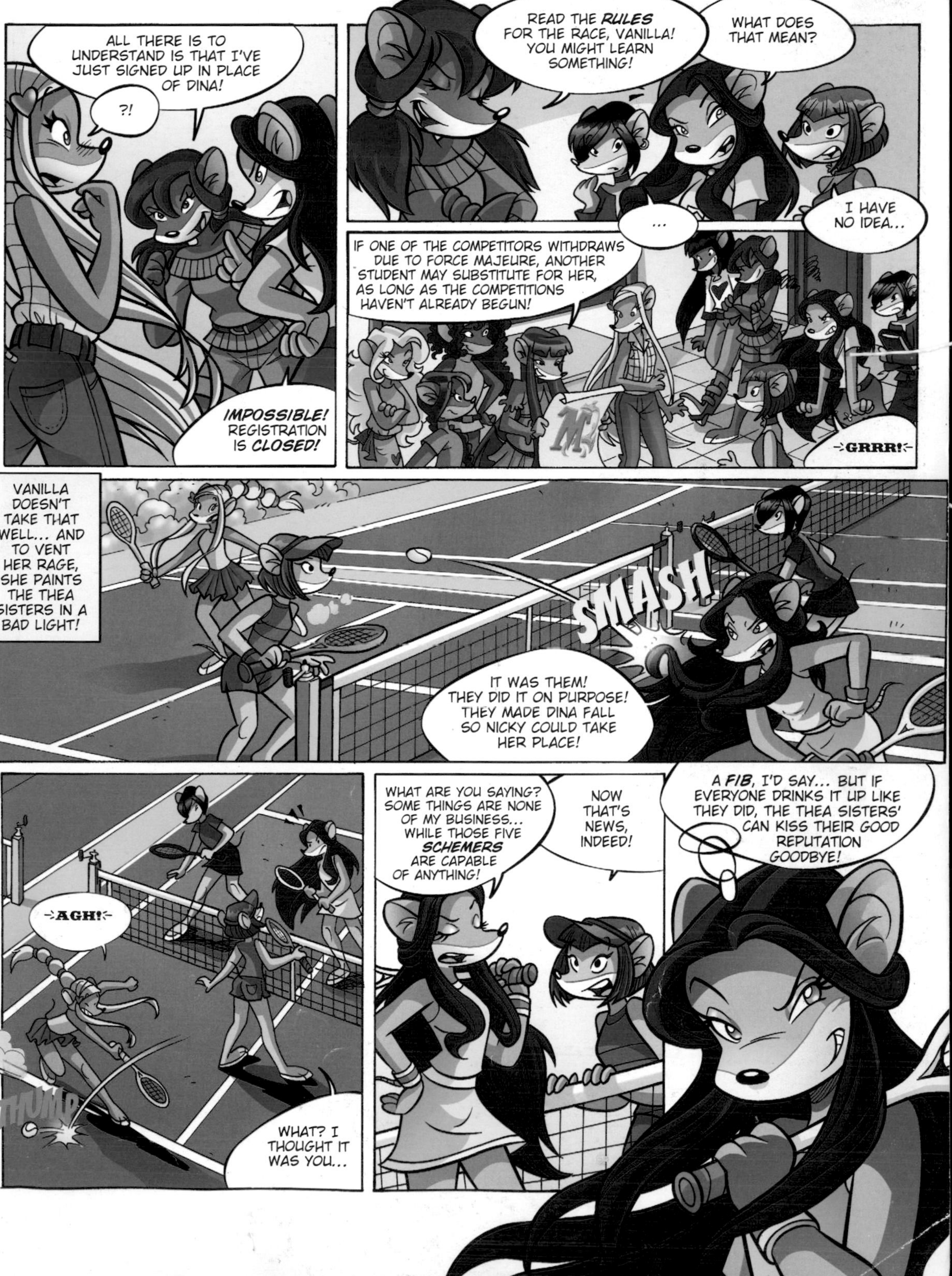

ALL THERE IS TO UNDERSTAND IS THAT I'VE JUST SIGNED UP IN PLACE OF DINA!
?!
IMPOSSIBLE! REGISTRATION IS CLOSED!
READ THE RULES FOR THE RACE, VANILLA! YOU MIGHT LEARN SOMETHING!
WHAT DOES THAT MEAN?
...
I HAVE NO IDEA...
IF ONE OF THE COMPETITORS WITHDRAWS DUE TO FORCE MAJEURE, ANOTHER STUDENT MAY SUBSTITUTE FOR HER, AS LONG AS THE COMPETITIONS HAVEN'T ALREADY BEGUN!
GRRR!
VANILLA DOESN'T TAKE THAT WELL... AND TO VENT HER RAGE, SHE PAINTS THE THEA SISTERS IN A BAD LIGHT!
SMASH
IT WAS THEM! THEY DID IT ON PURPOSE! THEY MADE DINA FALL SO NICKY COULD TAKE HER PLACE!
AGH!
THUMP
WHAT? I THOUGHT IT WAS YOU...
WHAT ARE YOU SAYING? SOME THINGS ARE NONE OF MY BUSINESS... WHILE THOSE FIVE SCHEMERS ARE CAPABLE OF ANYTHING!
NOW THAT'S NEWS, INDEED!
A FIB, I'D SAY... BUT IF EVERYONE DRINKS IT UP LIKE THEY DID, THE THEA SISTERS' CAN KISS THEIR GOOD REPUTATION GOODBYE!

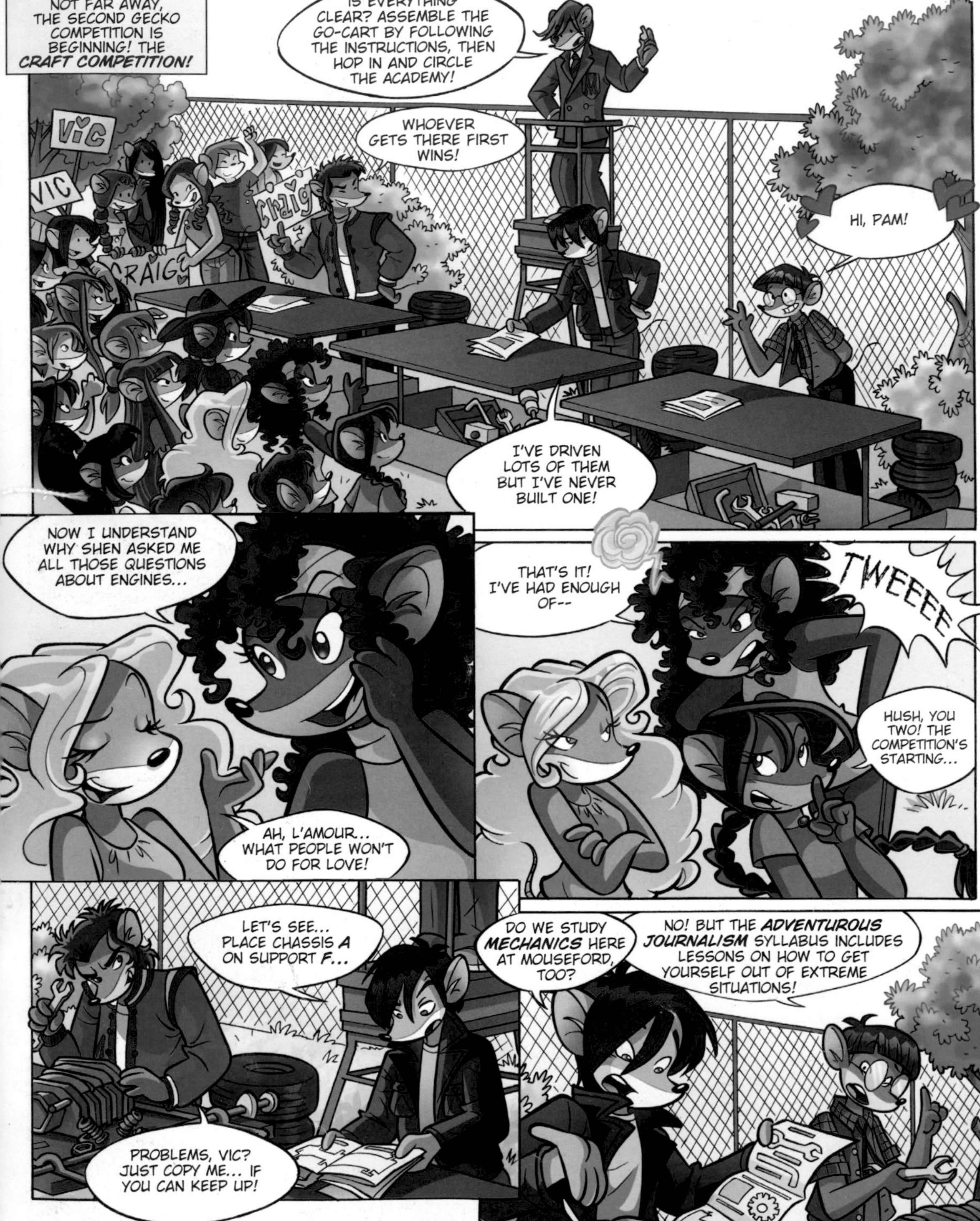
NOT FAR AWAY, THE SECOND GECKO COMPETITION IS BEGINNING! THE CRAFT COMPETITION!
IS EVERYTHING CLEAR? ASSEMBLE THE GO-CART BY FOLLOWING THE INSTRUCTIONS, THEN HOP IN AND CIRCLE THE ACADEMY!
WHOEVER GETS THERE FIRST WINS!
VIC
VIC
CRAIG
CRAIG
HI, PAM!
I'VE DRIVEN LOTS OF THEM BUT I'VE NEVER BUILT ONE!
NOW I UNDERSTAND WHY SHEN ASKED ME ALL THOSE QUESTIONS ABOUT ENGINES...
AH, L'AMOUR... WHAT PEOPLE WON'T DO FOR LOVE!
THAT'S IT! I'VE HAD ENOUGH OF--
TWEEEE
HUSH, YOU TWO! THE COMPETITION'S STARTING...
LET'S SEE... PLACE CHASSIS A ON SUPPORT F...
PROBLEMS, VIC? JUST COPY ME... IF YOU CAN KEEP UP!
DO WE STUDY MECHANICS HERE AT MOUSEFORD, TOO?
NO! BUT THE ADVENTUROUS JOURNALISM SYLLABUS INCLUDES LESSONS ON HOW TO GET YOURSELF OUT OF EXTREME SITUATIONS!

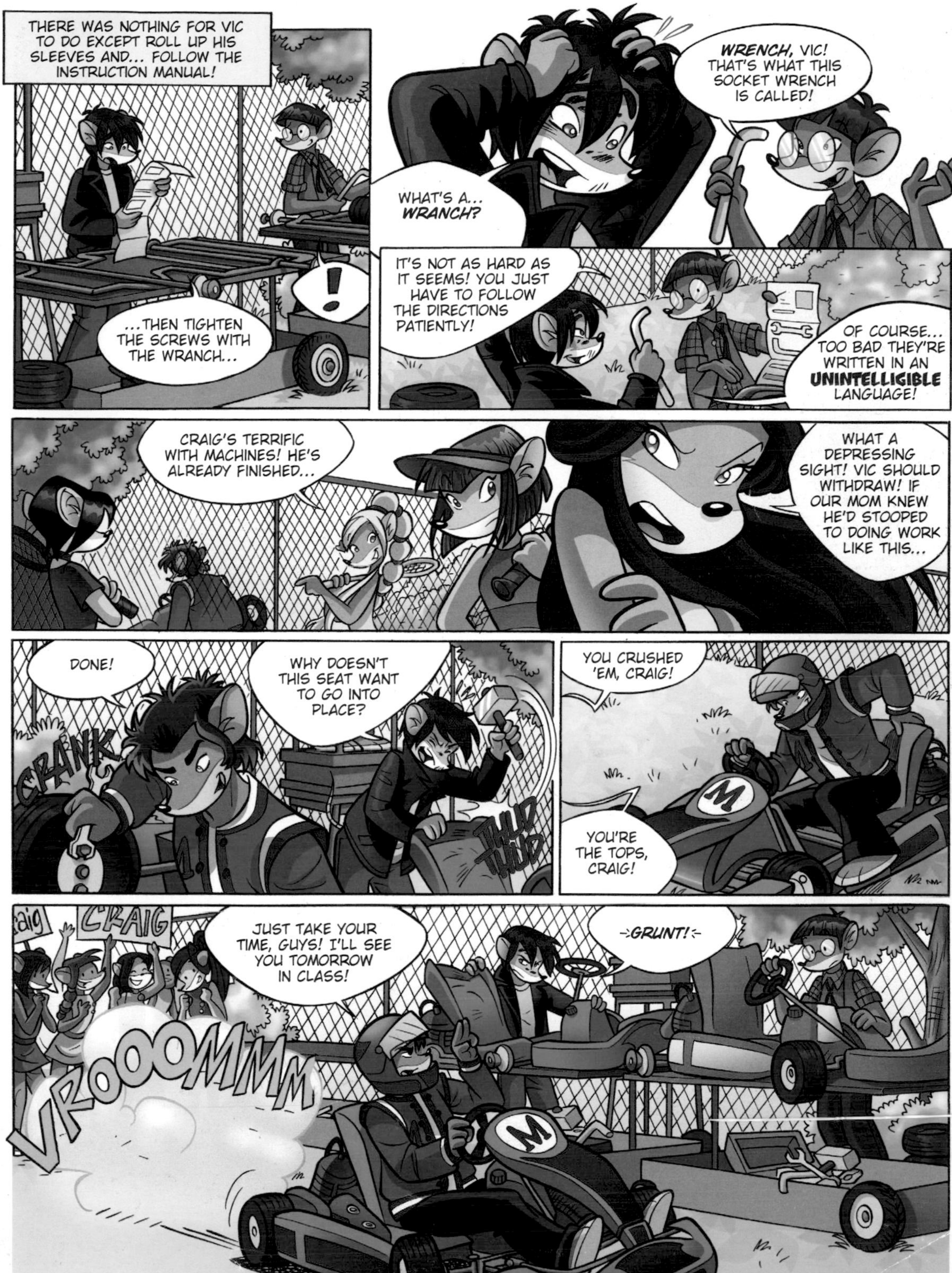
THERE WAS NOTHING FOR VIC TO DO EXCEPT ROLL UP HIS SLEEVES AND... FOLLOW THE INSTRUCTION MANUAL!
...THEN TIGHTEN THE SCREWS WITH THE WRANCH...
!
WHAT'S A... WRANCH?
WRENCH, VIC! THAT'S WHAT THIS SOCKET WRENCH IS CALLED!
IT'S NOT AS HARD AS IT SEEMS! YOU JUST HAVE TO FOLLOW THE DIRECTIONS PATIENTLY!
OF COURSE... TOO BAD THEY'RE WRITTEN IN AN UNINTELLIGIBLE LANGUAGE!
CRAIG'S TERRIFIC WITH MACHINES! HE'S ALREADY FINISHED...
WHAT A DEPRESSING SIGHT! VIC SHOULD WITHDRAW! IF OUR MOM KNEW HE'D STOOPED TO DOING WORK LIKE THIS...
DONE!
CRANK
WHY DOESN'T THIS SEAT WANT TO GO INTO PLACE?
THUD THUD
YOU CRUSHED 'EM, CRAIG!
YOU'RE THE TOPS, CRAIG!
CRAIG
JUST TAKE YOUR TIME, GUYS! I'LL SEE YOU TOMORROW IN CLASS!
-GRUNT!-
VROOOMMMM

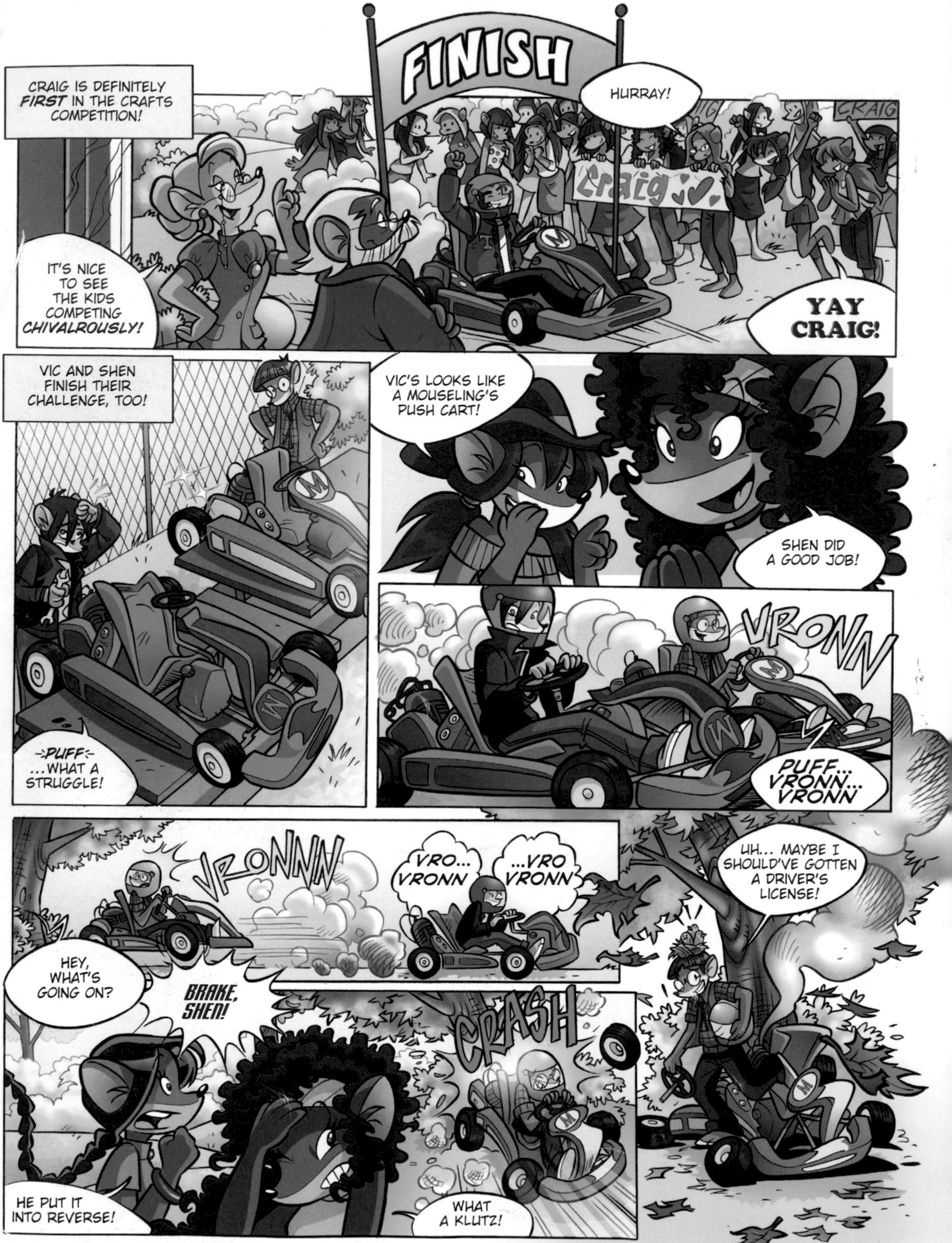
FINISH
CRAIG IS DEFINITELY FIRST IN THE CRAFTS COMPETITION!
HURRAY!
CRAIG
Craig
IT'S NICE TO SEE THE KIDS COMPETING CHIVALROUSLY!
YAY CRAIG!
VIC AND SHEN FINISH THEIR CHALLENGE, TOO!
VIC'S LOOKS LIKE A MOUSELING'S PUSH CART!
SHEN DID A GOOD JOB!
PUFF ...WHAT A STRUGGLE!
VRONN
PUFF... VRONN... VRONN
VRONNN
VRO... VRONN
...VRO VRONN
UH... MAYBE I SHOULD'VE GOTTEN A DRIVER'S LICENSE!
HEY, WHAT'S GOING ON?
BRAKE, SHEN!
CRASH
HE PUT IT INTO REVERSE!
WHAT A KLUTZ!

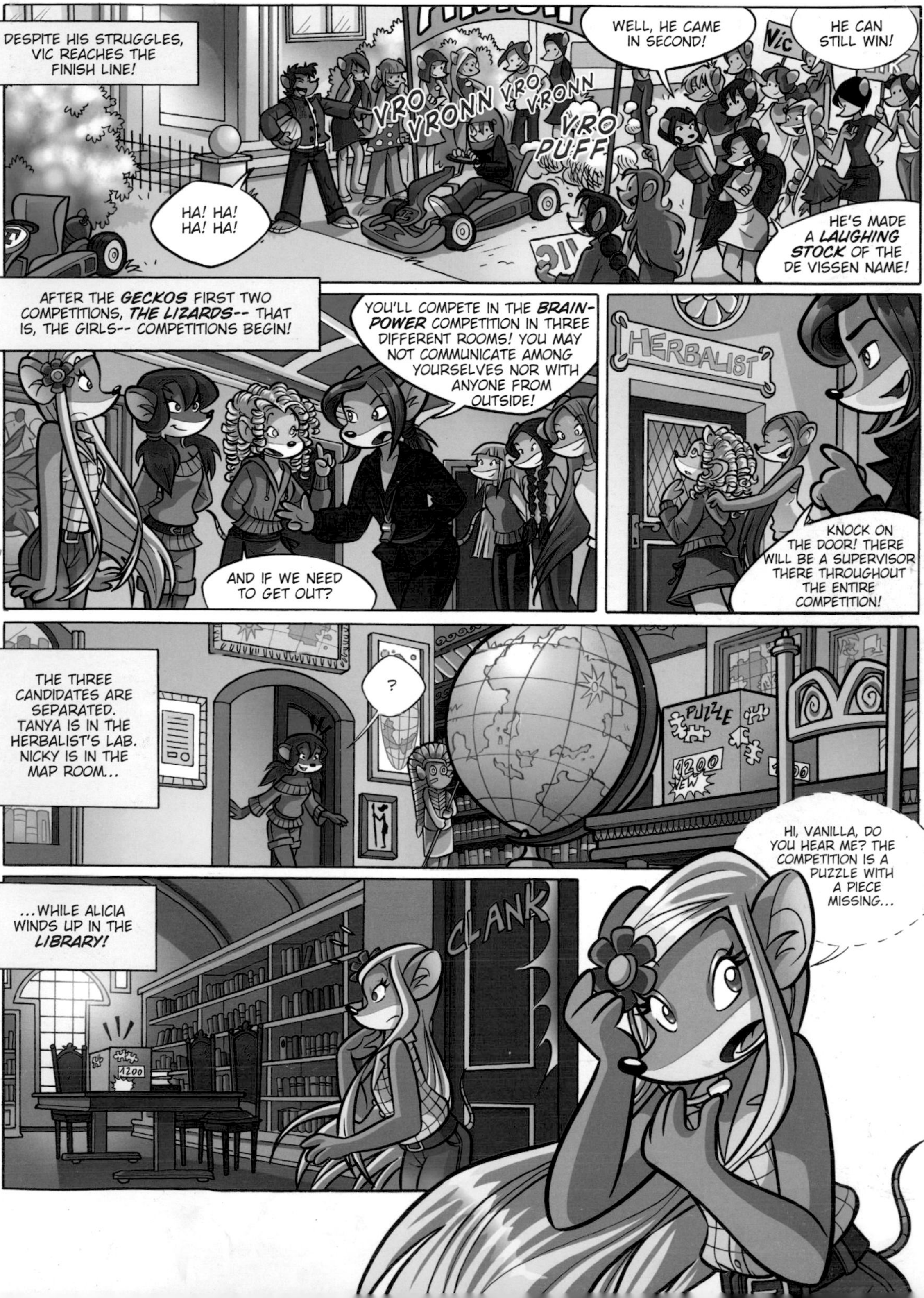
DESPITE HIS STRUGGLES, VIC REACHES THE FINISH LINE!
WELL, HE CAME IN SECOND!
HE CAN STILL WIN!
VRO VRONN VRO VRONN VRO PUFF
HA! HA! HA! HA!
HE'S MADE A **LAUGHING STOCK** OF THE DE VISSEN NAME!
AFTER THE **GECKOS** FIRST TWO COMPETITIONS, **THE LIZARDS--** THAT IS, THE GIRLS-- COMPETITIONS BEGIN!
YOU'LL COMPETE IN THE **BRAIN-POWER** COMPETITION IN THREE DIFFERENT ROOMS! YOU MAY NOT COMMUNICATE AMONG YOURSELVES NOR WITH ANYONE FROM OUTSIDE!
AND IF WE NEED TO GET OUT?
HERBALIST
KNOCK ON THE DOOR! THERE WILL BE A SUPERVISOR THERE THROUGHOUT THE ENTIRE COMPETITION!
THE THREE CANDIDATES ARE SEPARATED. TANYA IS IN THE HERBALIST'S LAB. NICKY IS IN THE MAP ROOM...
?
PUZZLE
1200
NEW
HI, VANILLA, DO YOU HEAR ME? THE COMPETITION IS A PUZZLE WITH A PIECE MISSING...
...WHILE ALICIA WINDS UP IN THE **LIBRARY!**
CLANK
1200

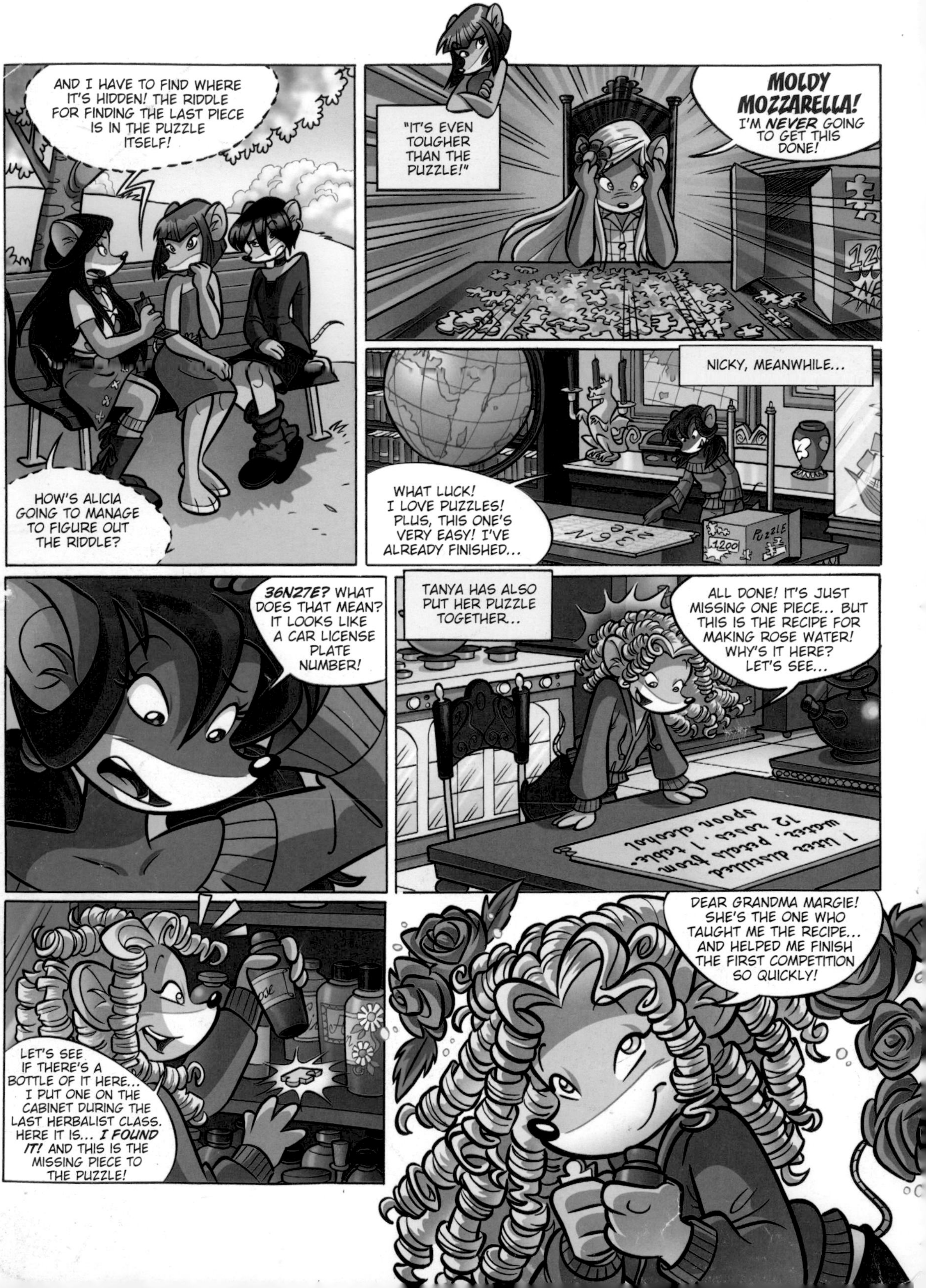
AND I HAVE TO FIND WHERE IT'S HIDDEN! THE RIDDLE FOR FINDING THE LAST PIECE IS IN THE PUZZLE ITSELF!
HOW'S ALICIA GOING TO MANAGE TO FIGURE OUT THE RIDDLE?
"IT'S EVEN TOUGHER THAN THE PUZZLE!"
MOLDY MOZZARELLA! I'M NEVER GOING TO GET THIS DONE!
NICKY, MEANWHILE...
WHAT LUCK! I LOVE PUZZLES! PLUS, THIS ONE'S VERY EASY! I'VE ALREADY FINISHED...
36N27E? WHAT DOES THAT MEAN? IT LOOKS LIKE A CAR LICENSE PLATE NUMBER!
TANYA HAS ALSO PUT HER PUZZLE TOGETHER...
ALL DONE! IT'S JUST MISSING ONE PIECE... BUT THIS IS THE RECIPE FOR MAKING ROSE WATER! WHY'S IT HERE? LET'S SEE...
1 liter distilled water, petals from 12 roses, 1 table-spoon alcohol
LET'S SEE IF THERE'S A BOTTLE OF IT HERE... I PUT ONE ON THE CABINET DURING THE LAST HERBALIST CLASS. HERE IT IS... I FOUND IT! AND THIS IS THE MISSING PIECE TO THE PUZZLE!
DEAR GRANDMA MARGIE! SHE'S THE ONE WHO TAUGHT ME THE RECIPE... AND HELPED ME FINISH THE FIRST COMPETITION SO QUICKLY!

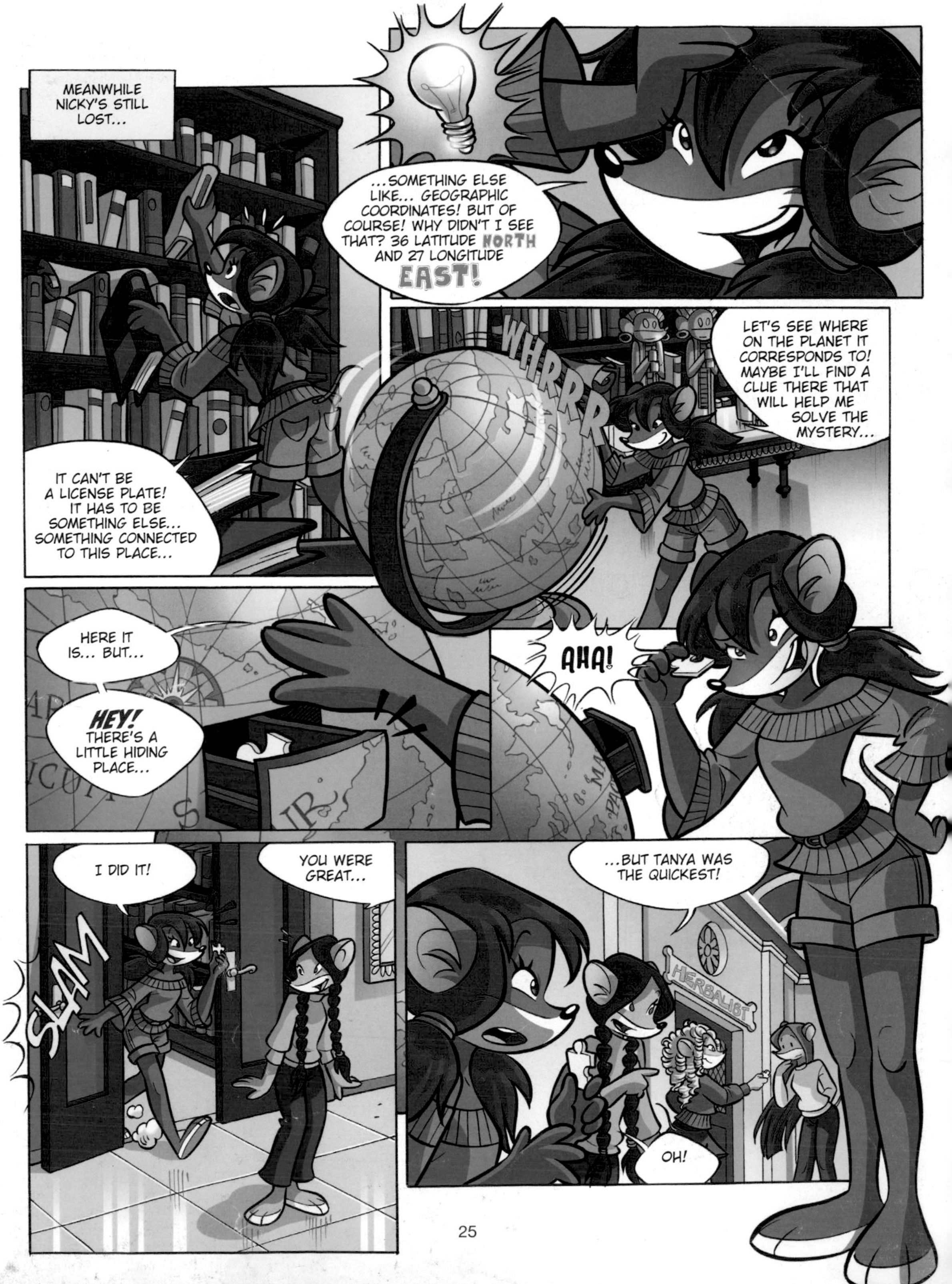

MEANWHILE NICKY'S STILL LOST...
IT CAN'T BE A LICENSE PLATE! IT HAS TO BE SOMETHING ELSE... SOMETHING CONNECTED TO THIS PLACE...
...SOMETHING ELSE LIKE... GEOGRAPHIC COORDINATES! BUT OF COURSE! WHY DIDN'T I SEE THAT? 36 LATITUDE NORTH AND 27 LONGITUDE EAST!
WHRRRR
LET'S SEE WHERE ON THE PLANET IT CORRESPONDS TO! MAYBE I'LL FIND A CLUE THERE THAT WILL HELP ME SOLVE THE MYSTERY...
HERE IT IS... BUT...
HEY! THERE'S A LITTLE HIDING PLACE...
AHA!
I DID IT!
SLAM
YOU WERE GREAT...
...BUT TANYA WAS THE QUICKEST!
HERBALIST
OH!

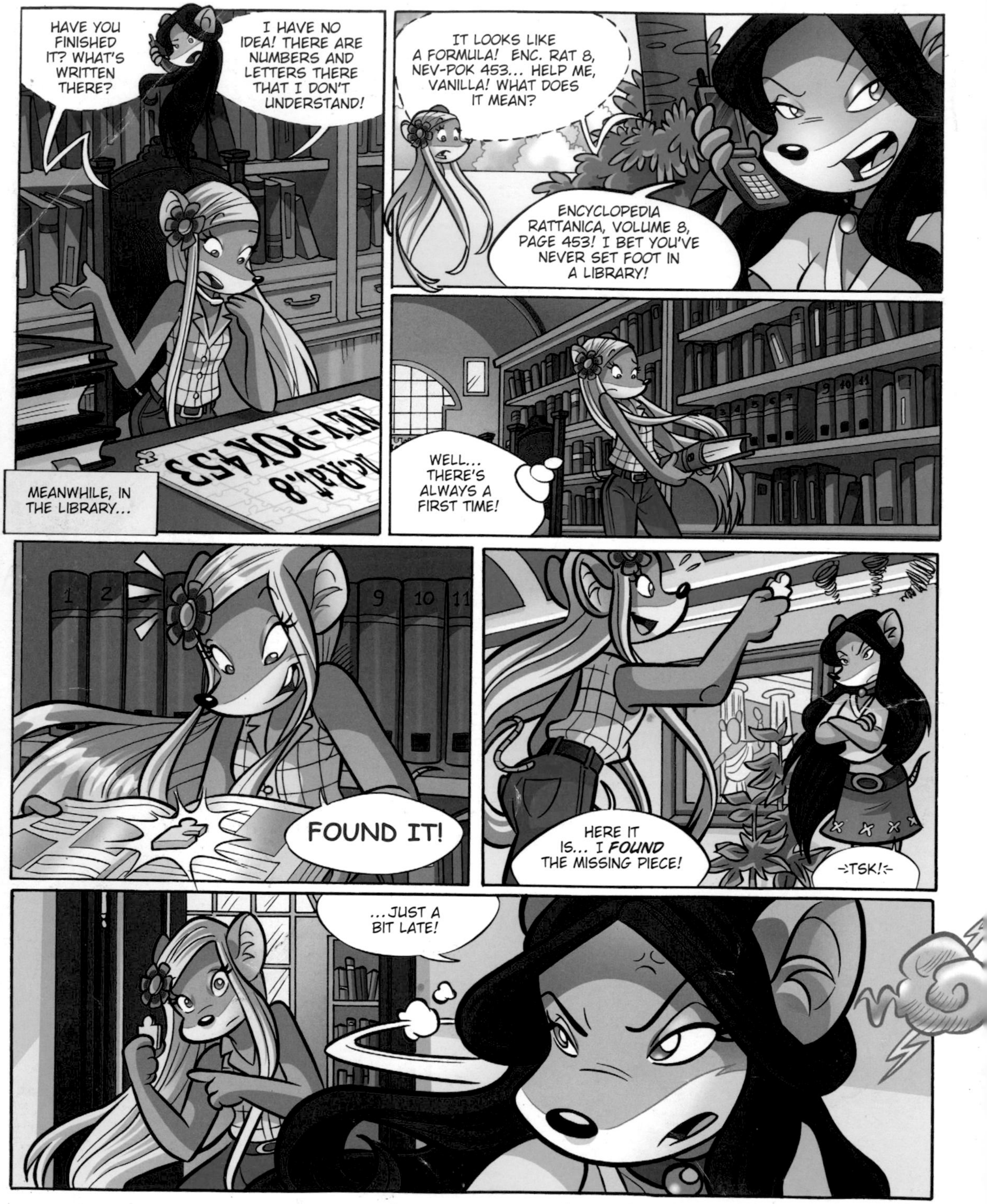

HAVE YOU FINISHED IT? WHAT'S WRITTEN THERE?
I HAVE NO IDEA! THERE ARE NUMBERS AND LETTERS THERE THAT I DON'T UNDERSTAND!
MEANWHILE, IN THE LIBRARY...
IT LOOKS LIKE A FORMULA! ENC. RAT 8, NEV-POK 453... HELP ME, VANILLA! WHAT DOES IT MEAN?
ENCYCLOPEDIA RATTANICA, VOLUME 8, PAGE 453! I BET YOU'VE NEVER SET FOOT IN A LIBRARY!
WELL... THERE'S ALWAYS A FIRST TIME!
FOUND IT!
HERE IT IS... I FOUND THE MISSING PIECE!
TSK!
...JUST A BIT LATE!

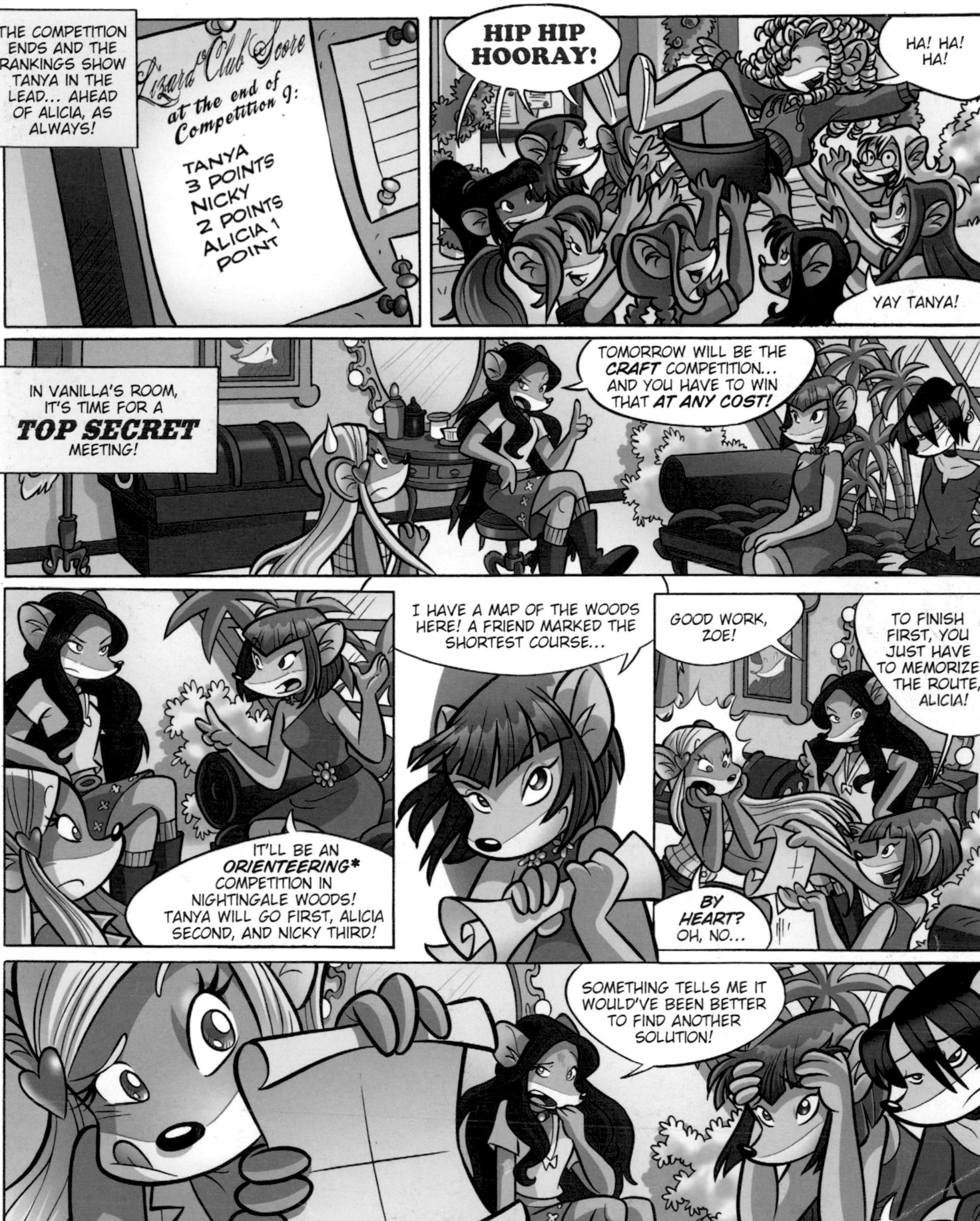
THE COMPETITION ENDS AND THE RANKINGS SHOW TANYA IN THE LEAD... AHEAD OF ALICIA, AS ALWAYS!
Lizard Club Score at the end of Competition 9:
TANYA 3 POINTS NICKY 2 POINTS ALICIA 1 POINT
HIP HIP HOORAY!
HA! HA! HA!
YAY TANYA!
IN VANILLA'S ROOM, IT'S TIME FOR A TOP SECRET MEETING!
TOMORROW WILL BE THE CRAFT COMPETITION... AND YOU HAVE TO WIN THAT AT ANY COST!
IT'LL BE AN ORIENTEERING* COMPETITION IN NIGHTINGALE WOODS! TANYA WILL GO FIRST, ALICIA SECOND, AND NICKY THIRD!
I HAVE A MAP OF THE WOODS HERE! A FRIEND MARKED THE SHORTEST COURSE...
GOOD WORK, ZOE!
TO FINISH FIRST, YOU JUST HAVE TO MEMORIZE THE ROUTE, ALICIA!
BY HEART? OH, NO...
SOMETHING TELLS ME IT WOULD'VE BEEN BETTER TO FIND ANOTHER SOLUTION!
-SIGH-...
...

*A SPORT IN WHICH COMPETITORS NAVIGATE UNFAMILIAR TERRAIN USING A MAP AND A COMPASS!

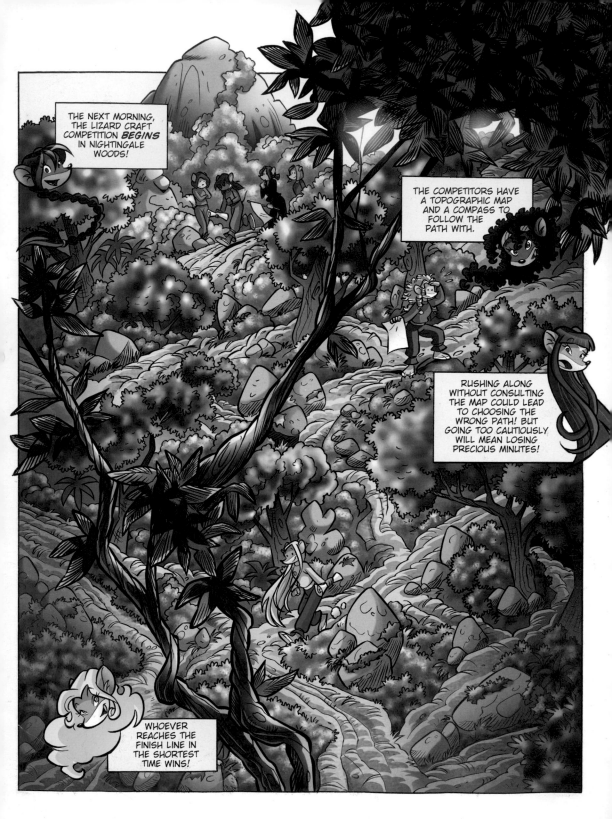

THE NEXT MORNING, THE LIZARD CRAFT COMPETITION *BEGINS* IN NIGHTINGALE WOODS!

THE COMPETITORS HAVE A TOPOGRAPHIC MAP AND A COMPASS TO FOLLOW THE PATH WITH.

RUSHING ALONG WITHOUT CONSULTING THE MAP COULD LEAD TO CHOOSING THE WRONG PATH! BUT GOING TOO CAUTIOUSLY WILL MEAN LOSING PRECIOUS MINUTES!

WHOEVER REACHES THE FINISH LINE IN THE SHORTEST TIME WINS!

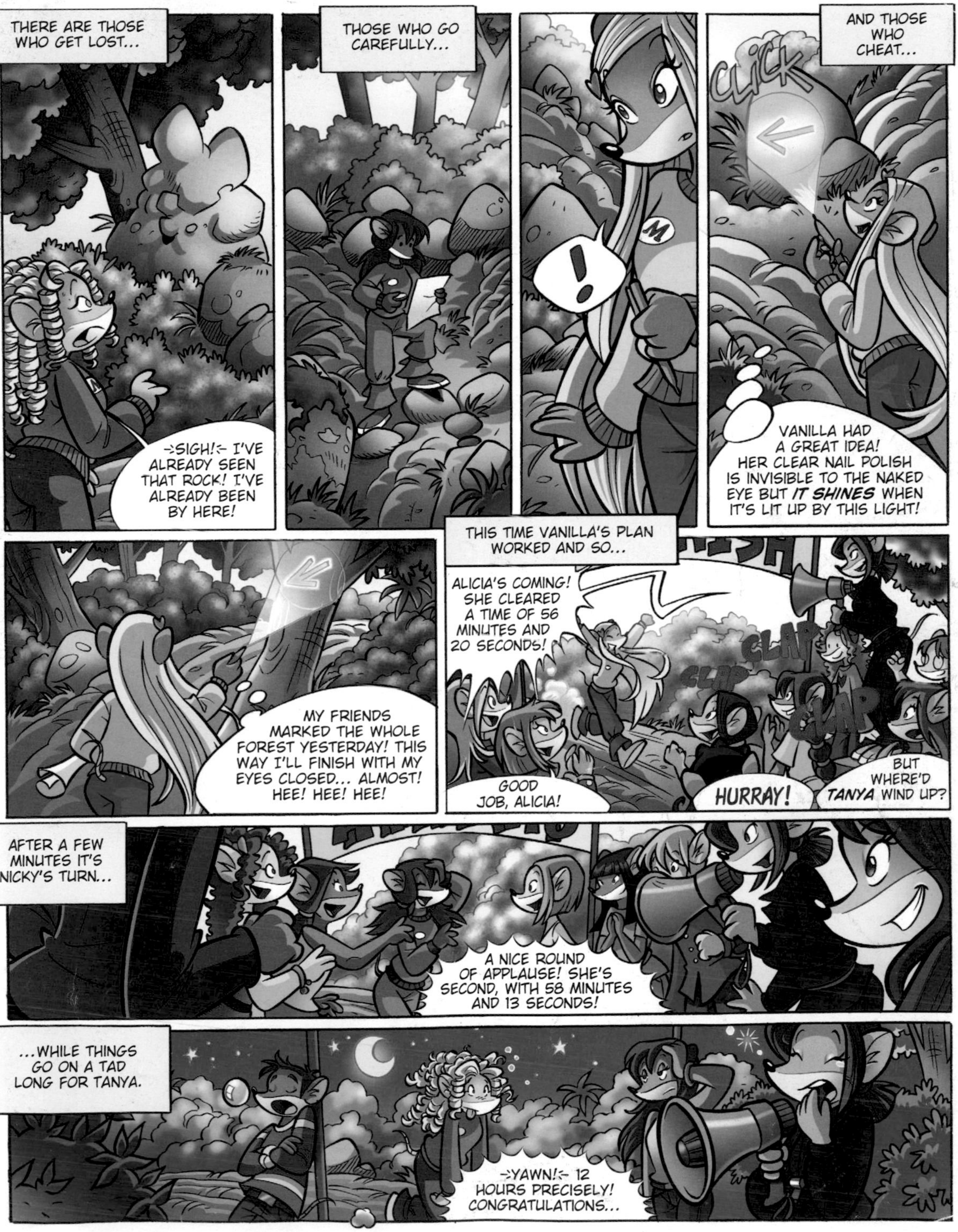
THERE ARE THOSE WHO GET LOST...
→SIGH!← I'VE ALREADY SEEN THAT ROCK! I'VE ALREADY BEEN BY HERE!
THOSE WHO GO CAREFULLY...
!
AND THOSE WHO CHEAT...
CLICK
VANILLA HAD A GREAT IDEA! HER CLEAR NAIL POLISH IS INVISIBLE TO THE NAKED EYE BUT IT SHINES WHEN IT'S LIT UP BY THIS LIGHT!
MY FRIENDS MARKED THE WHOLE FOREST YESTERDAY! THIS WAY I'LL FINISH WITH MY EYES CLOSED... ALMOST! HEE! HEE! HEE!
THIS TIME VANILLA'S PLAN WORKED AND SO...
ALICIA'S COMING! SHE CLEARED A TIME OF 56 MINUTES AND 20 SECONDS!
CLAP
CLAP
CLAP
GOOD JOB, ALICIA!
HURRAY!
BUT WHERE'D TANYA WIND UP?
AFTER A FEW MINUTES IT'S NICKY'S TURN...
A NICE ROUND OF APPLAUSE! SHE'S SECOND, WITH 58 MINUTES AND 13 SECONDS!
...WHILE THINGS GO ON A TAD LONG FOR TANYA.
→YAWN!← 12 HOURS PRECISELY! CONGRATULATIONS...

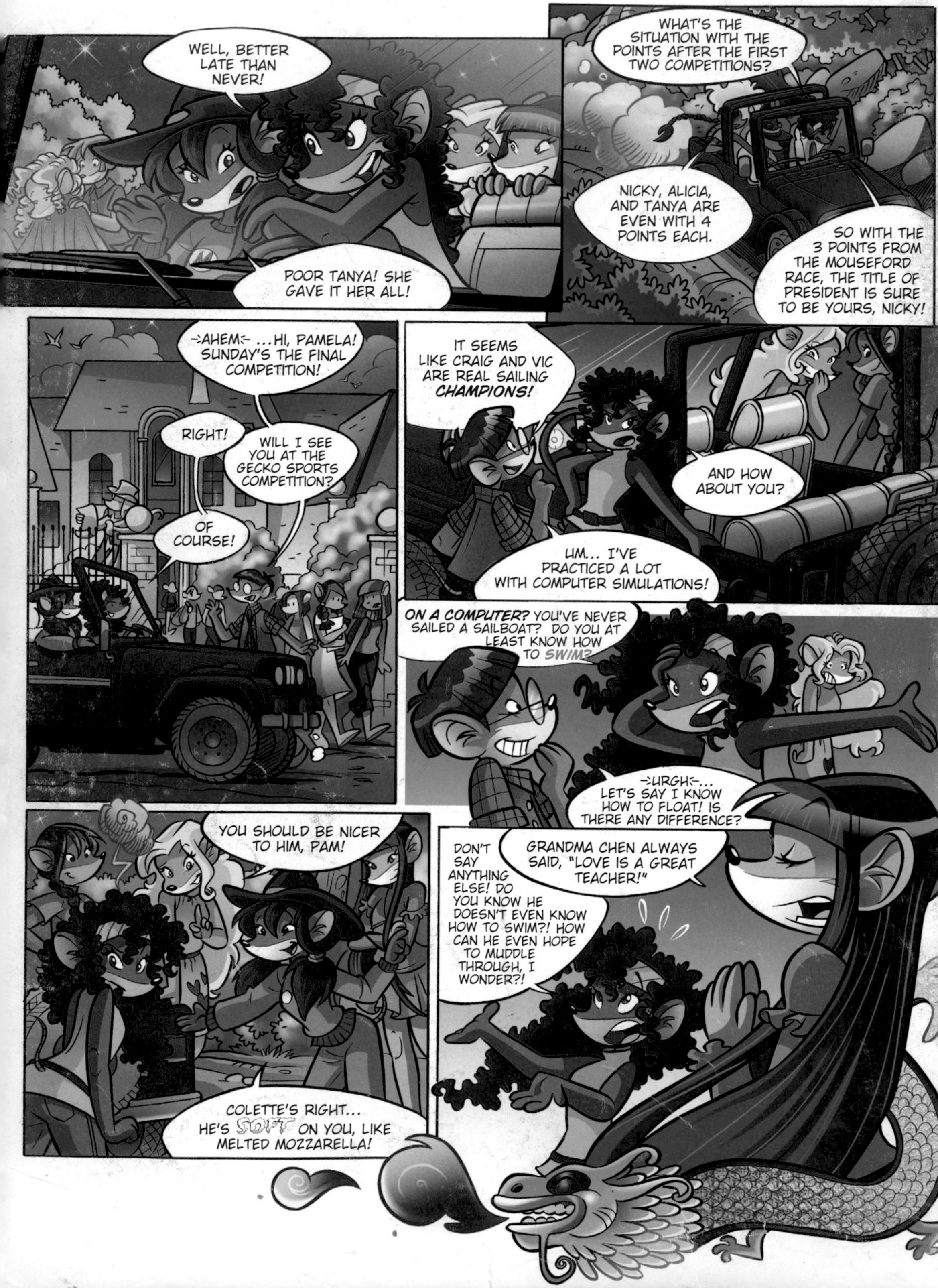
WELL, BETTER LATE THAN NEVER!
POOR TANYA! SHE GAVE IT HER ALL!
WHAT'S THE SITUATION WITH THE POINTS AFTER THE FIRST TWO COMPETITIONS?
NICKY, ALICIA, AND TANYA ARE EVEN WITH 4 POINTS EACH.
SO WITH THE 3 POINTS FROM THE MOUSEFORD RACE, THE TITLE OF PRESIDENT IS SURE TO BE YOURS, NICKY!
-AHEM- ...HI, PAMELA! SUNDAY'S THE FINAL COMPETITION!
RIGHT!
WILL I SEE YOU AT THE GECKO SPORTS COMPETITION?
OF COURSE!
IT SEEMS LIKE CRAIG AND VIC ARE REAL SAILING CHAMPIONS!
AND HOW ABOUT YOU?
UM... I'VE PRACTICED A LOT WITH COMPUTER SIMULATIONS!
ON A COMPUTER? YOU'VE NEVER SAILED A SAILBOAT? DO YOU AT LEAST KNOW HOW TO SWIM?
-URGH-... LET'S SAY I KNOW HOW TO FLOAT! IS THERE ANY DIFFERENCE?
YOU SHOULD BE NICER TO HIM, PAM!
COLETTE'S RIGHT... HE'S SOFT ON YOU, LIKE MELTED MOZZARELLA!
GRANDMA CHEN ALWAYS SAID, "LOVE IS A GREAT TEACHER!"
DON'T SAY ANYTHING ELSE! DO YOU KNOW HE DOESN'T EVEN KNOW HOW TO SWIM?! HOW CAN HE EVEN HOPE TO MUDDLE THROUGH, I WONDER?!

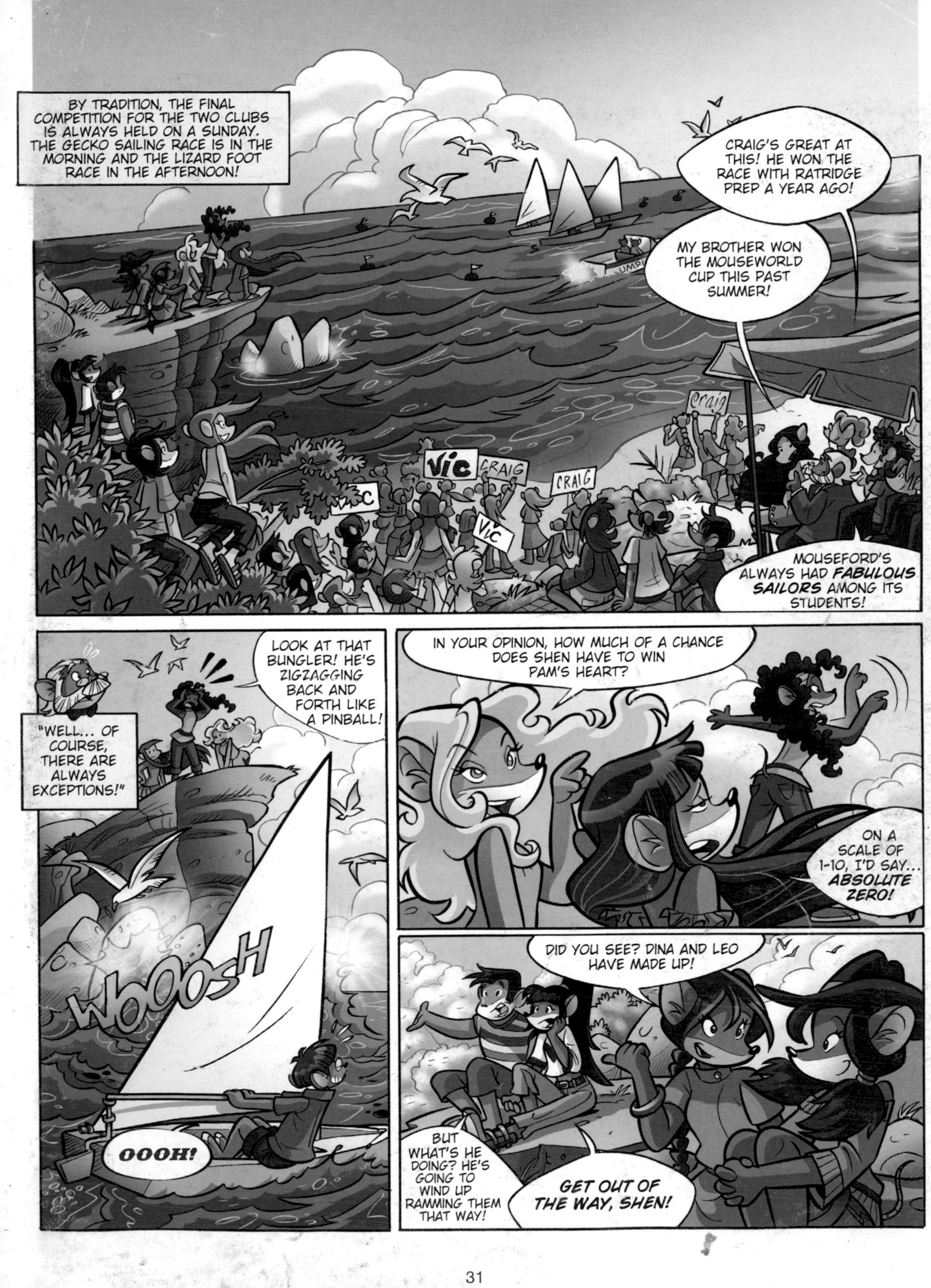
BY TRADITION, THE FINAL COMPETITION FOR THE TWO CLUBS IS ALWAYS HELD ON A SUNDAY. THE GECKO SAILING RACE IS IN THE MORNING AND THE LIZARD FOOT RACE IN THE AFTERNOON!
CRAIG'S GREAT AT THIS! HE WON THE RACE WITH RATRIDGE PREP A YEAR AGO!
MY BROTHER WON THE MOUSEWORLD CUP THIS PAST SUMMER!
VIC
CRAIG
CRAIG
VIC
Craig
MOUSEFORD'S ALWAYS HAD **FABULOUS SAILORS** AMONG ITS STUDENTS!
LOOK AT THAT BUNGLER! HE'S ZIGZAGGING BACK AND FORTH LIKE A PINBALL!
"WELL... OF COURSE, THERE ARE ALWAYS EXCEPTIONS!"
WOOOSH
OOOH!
IN YOUR OPINION, HOW MUCH OF A CHANCE DOES SHEN HAVE TO WIN PAM'S HEART?
ON A SCALE OF 1-10, I'D SAY... **ABSOLUTE ZERO!**
DID YOU SEE? DINA AND LEO HAVE MADE UP!
BUT WHAT'S HE DOING? HE'S GOING TO WIND UP RAMMING THEM THAT WAY!
GET OUT OF THE WAY, SHEN!

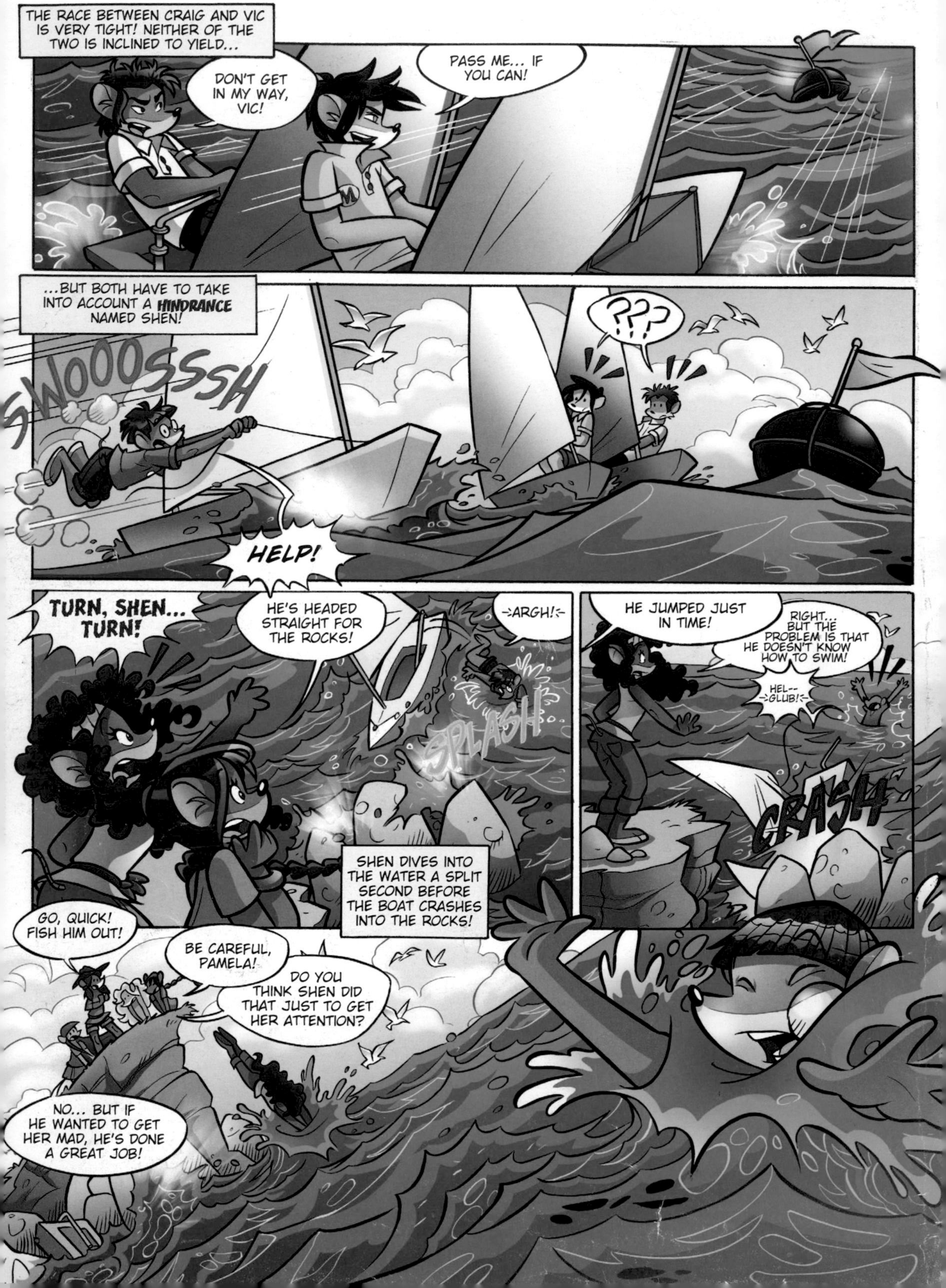

THE RACE BETWEEN CRAIG AND VIC IS VERY TIGHT! NEITHER OF THE TWO IS INCLINED TO YIELD...
DON'T GET IN MY WAY, VIC!
PASS ME... IF YOU CAN!
...BUT BOTH HAVE TO TAKE INTO ACCOUNT A HINDRANCE NAMED SHEN!
SWOOOSSSH
???
HELP!
TURN, SHEN... TURN!
HE'S HEADED STRAIGHT FOR THE ROCKS!
ARGH!
SPLASH
HE JUMPED JUST IN TIME!
RIGHT... BUT THE PROBLEM IS THAT HE DOESN'T KNOW HOW TO SWIM!
HEL-- GLUB!
CRASH
SHEN DIVES INTO THE WATER A SPLIT SECOND BEFORE THE BOAT CRASHES INTO THE ROCKS!
GO, QUICK! FISH HIM OUT!
BE CAREFUL, PAMELA!
DO YOU THINK SHEN DID THAT JUST TO GET HER ATTENTION?
NO... BUT IF HE WANTED TO GET HER MAD, HE'S DONE A GREAT JOB!

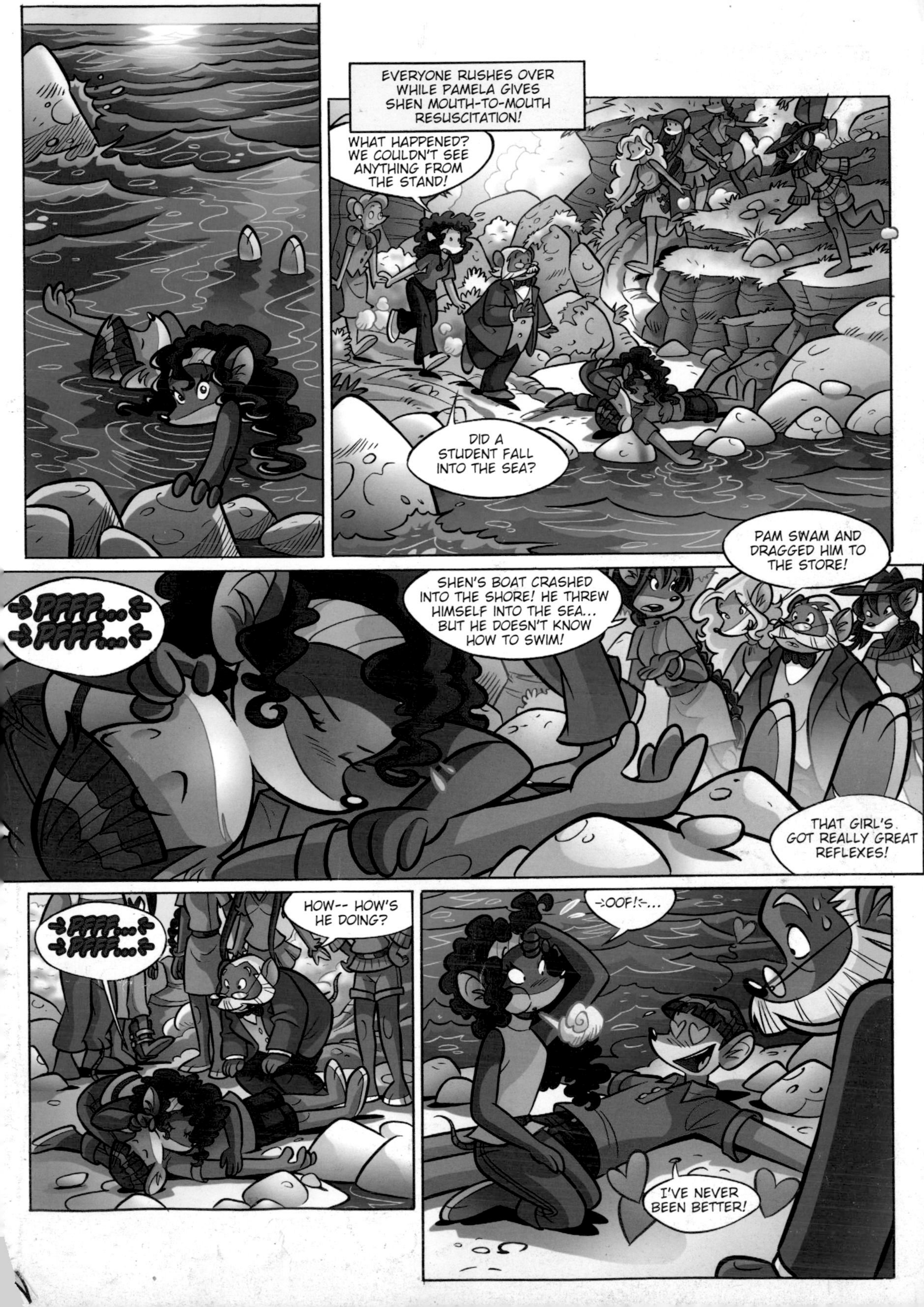
EVERYONE RUSHES OVER WHILE PAMELA GIVES SHEN MOUTH-TO-MOUTH RESUSCITATION!
WHAT HAPPENED? WE COULDN'T SEE ANYTHING FROM THE STAND!
DID A STUDENT FALL INTO THE SEA?
PFFF... PFFF...
SHEN'S BOAT CRASHED INTO THE SHORE! HE THREW HIMSELF INTO THE SEA... BUT HE DOESN'T KNOW HOW TO SWIM!
PAM SWAM AND DRAGGED HIM TO THE STORE!
THAT GIRL'S GOT REALLY GREAT REFLEXES!
PFFF... PFFF...
HOW-- HOW'S HE DOING?
OOF!...
I'VE NEVER BEEN BETTER!

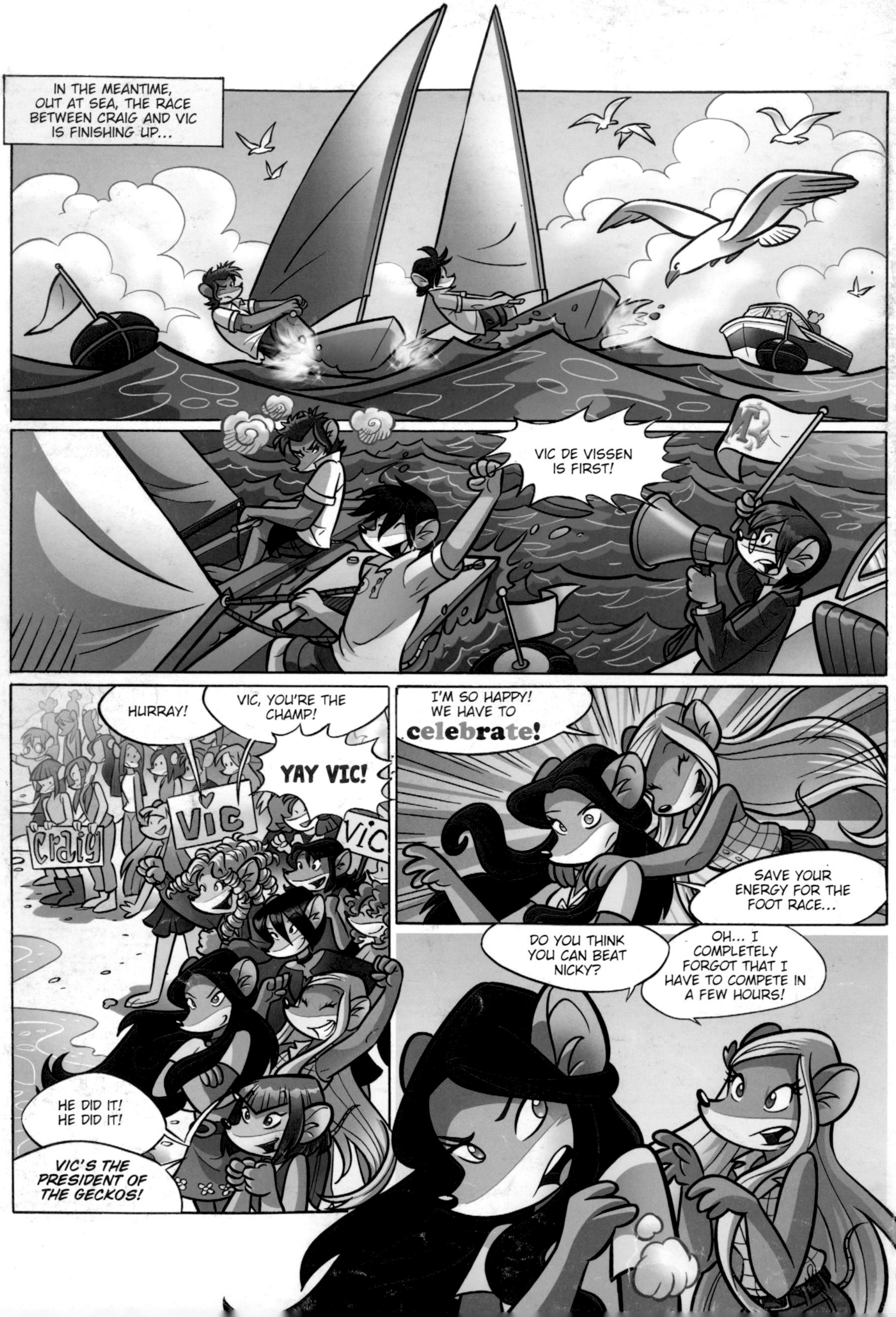

IN THE MEANTIME, OUT AT SEA, THE RACE BETWEEN CRAIG AND VIC IS FINISHING UP...
VIC DE VISSEN IS FIRST!
HURRAY!
VIC, YOU'RE THE CHAMP!
YAY VIC!
Vic
Craig
Vic
HE DID IT! HE DID IT!
VIC'S THE PRESIDENT OF THE GECKOS!
I'M SO HAPPY! WE HAVE TO celebrate!
SAVE YOUR ENERGY FOR THE FOOT RACE...
DO YOU THINK YOU CAN BEAT NICKY?
OH... I COMPLETELY FORGOT THAT I HAVE TO COMPETE IN A FEW HOURS!

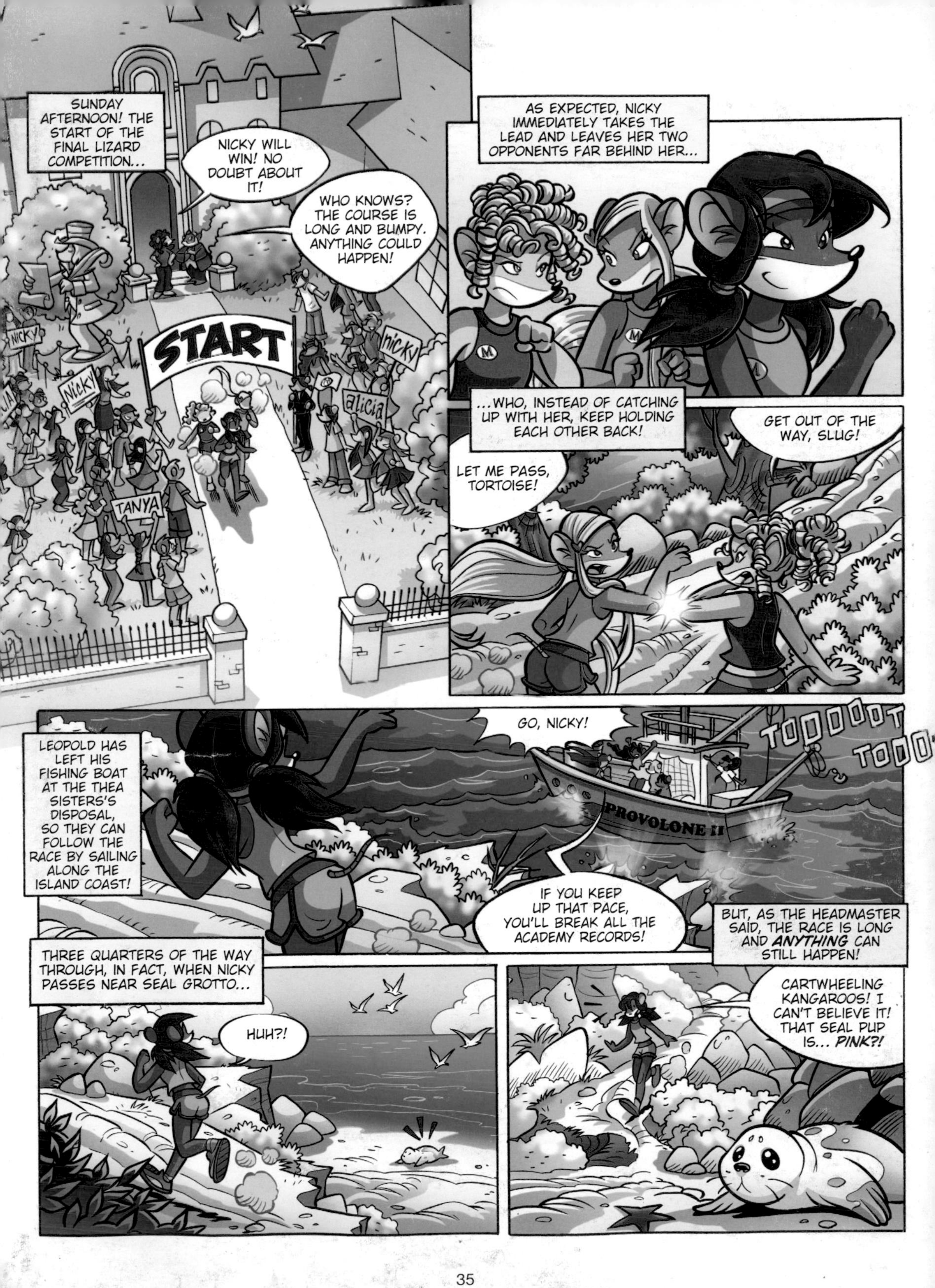
SUNDAY AFTERNOON! THE START OF THE FINAL LIZARD COMPETITION...
NICKY WILL WIN! NO DOUBT ABOUT IT!
WHO KNOWS? THE COURSE IS LONG AND BUMPY. ANYTHING COULD HAPPEN!
NICKY
START
NICKY
nicky
alicia
TANYA
AS EXPECTED, NICKY IMMEDIATELY TAKES THE LEAD AND LEAVES HER TWO OPPONENTS FAR BEHIND HER...
...WHO, INSTEAD OF CATCHING UP WITH HER, KEEP HOLDING EACH OTHER BACK!
GET OUT OF THE WAY, SLUG!
LET ME PASS, TORTOISE!
LEOPOLD HAS LEFT HIS FISHING BOAT AT THE THEA SISTERS'S DISPOSAL, SO THEY CAN FOLLOW THE RACE BY SAILING ALONG THE ISLAND COAST!
GO, NICKY!
TOOOOOT TOOO
PROVOLONE II
IF YOU KEEP UP THAT PACE, YOU'LL BREAK ALL THE ACADEMY RECORDS!
BUT, AS THE HEADMASTER SAID, THE RACE IS LONG AND ANYTHING CAN STILL HAPPEN!
THREE QUARTERS OF THE WAY THROUGH, IN FACT, WHEN NICKY PASSES NEAR SEAL GROTTO...
HUH?!
CARTWHEELING KANGAROOS! I CAN'T BELIEVE IT! THAT SEAL PUP IS... PINK?!

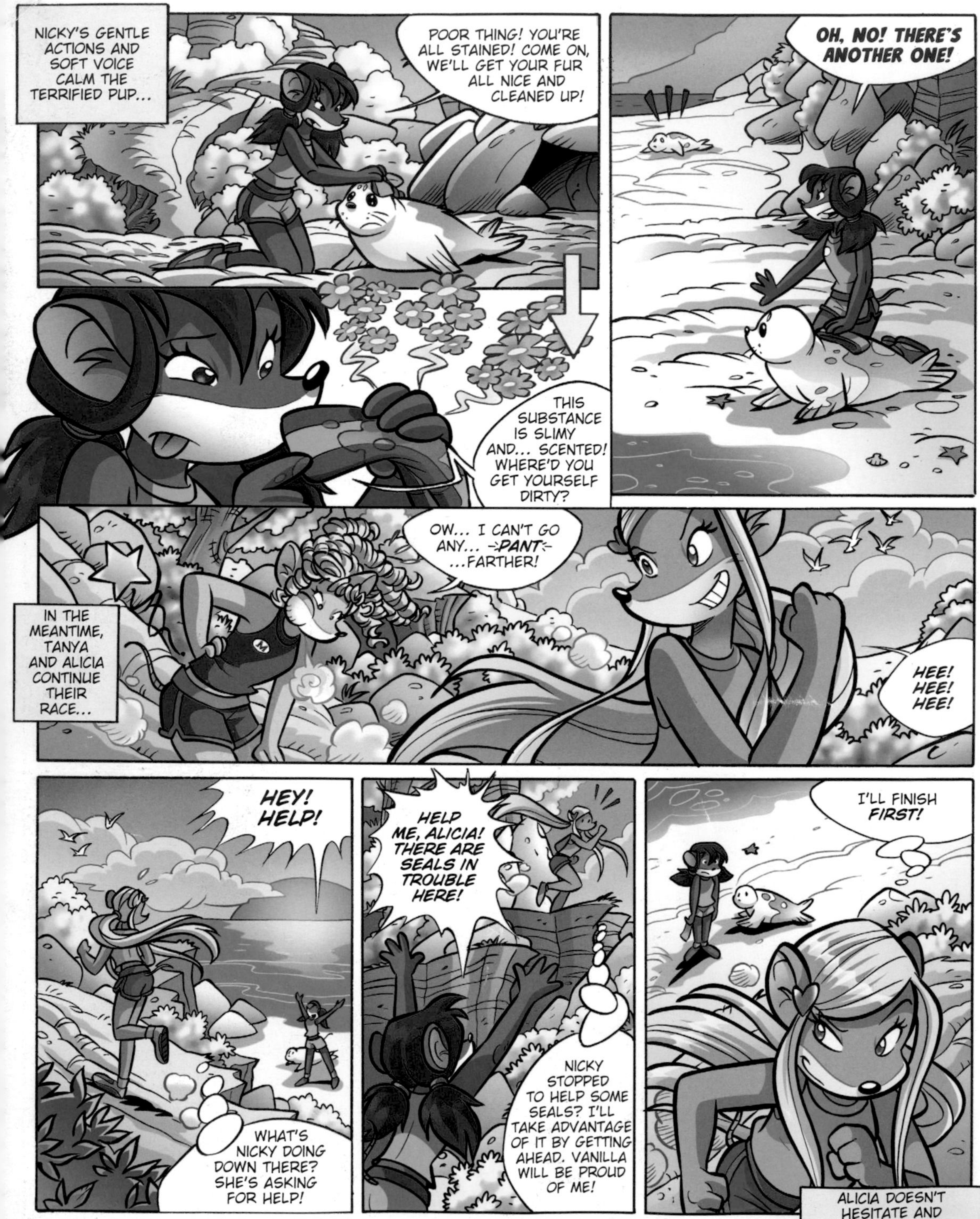
NICKY'S GENTLE ACTIONS AND SOFT VOICE CALM THE TERRIFIED PUP...
POOR THING! YOU'RE ALL STAINED! COME ON, WE'LL GET YOUR FUR ALL NICE AND CLEANED UP!
OH, NO! THERE'S ANOTHER ONE!
THIS SUBSTANCE IS SLIMY AND... SCENTED! WHERE'D YOU GET YOURSELF DIRTY?
IN THE MEANTIME, TANYA AND ALICIA CONTINUE THEIR RACE...
OW... I CAN'T GO ANY... PANT ...FARTHER!
HEE! HEE! HEE!
HEY! HELP!
WHAT'S NICKY DOING DOWN THERE? SHE'S ASKING FOR HELP!
HELP ME, ALICIA! THERE ARE SEALS IN TROUBLE HERE!
NICKY STOPPED TO HELP SOME SEALS? I'LL TAKE ADVANTAGE OF IT BY GETTING AHEAD. VANILLA WILL BE PROUD OF ME!
I'LL FINISH FIRST!
ALICIA DOESN'T HESITATE AND LENGTHENS HER STRIDE...

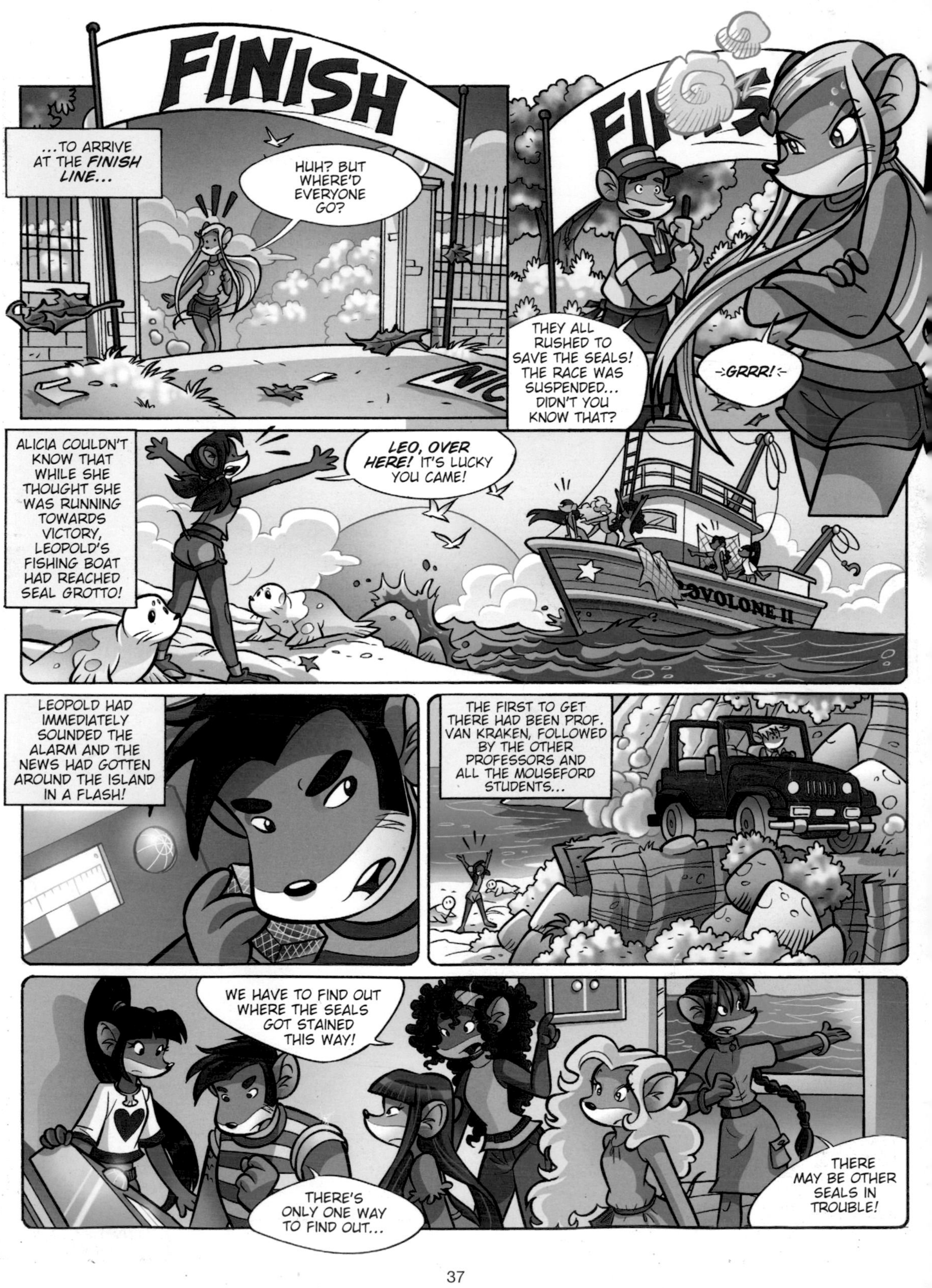
FINISH
...TO ARRIVE AT THE FINISH LINE...
HUH? BUT WHERE'D EVERYONE GO?
THEY ALL RUSHED TO SAVE THE SEALS! THE RACE WAS SUSPENDED... DIDN'T YOU KNOW THAT?
GRRR!
ALICIA COULDN'T KNOW THAT WHILE SHE THOUGHT SHE WAS RUNNING TOWARDS VICTORY, LEOPOLD'S FISHING BOAT HAD REACHED SEAL GROTTO!
LEO, OVER HERE! IT'S LUCKY YOU CAME!
LEOPOLD HAD IMMEDIATELY SOUNDED THE ALARM AND THE NEWS HAD GOTTEN AROUND THE ISLAND IN A FLASH!
THE FIRST TO GET THERE HAD BEEN PROF. VAN KRAKEN, FOLLOWED BY THE OTHER PROFESSORS AND ALL THE MOUSEFORD STUDENTS...
WE HAVE TO FIND OUT WHERE THE SEALS GOT STAINED THIS WAY!
THERE'S ONLY ONE WAY TO FIND OUT...
THERE MAY BE OTHER SEALS IN TROUBLE!

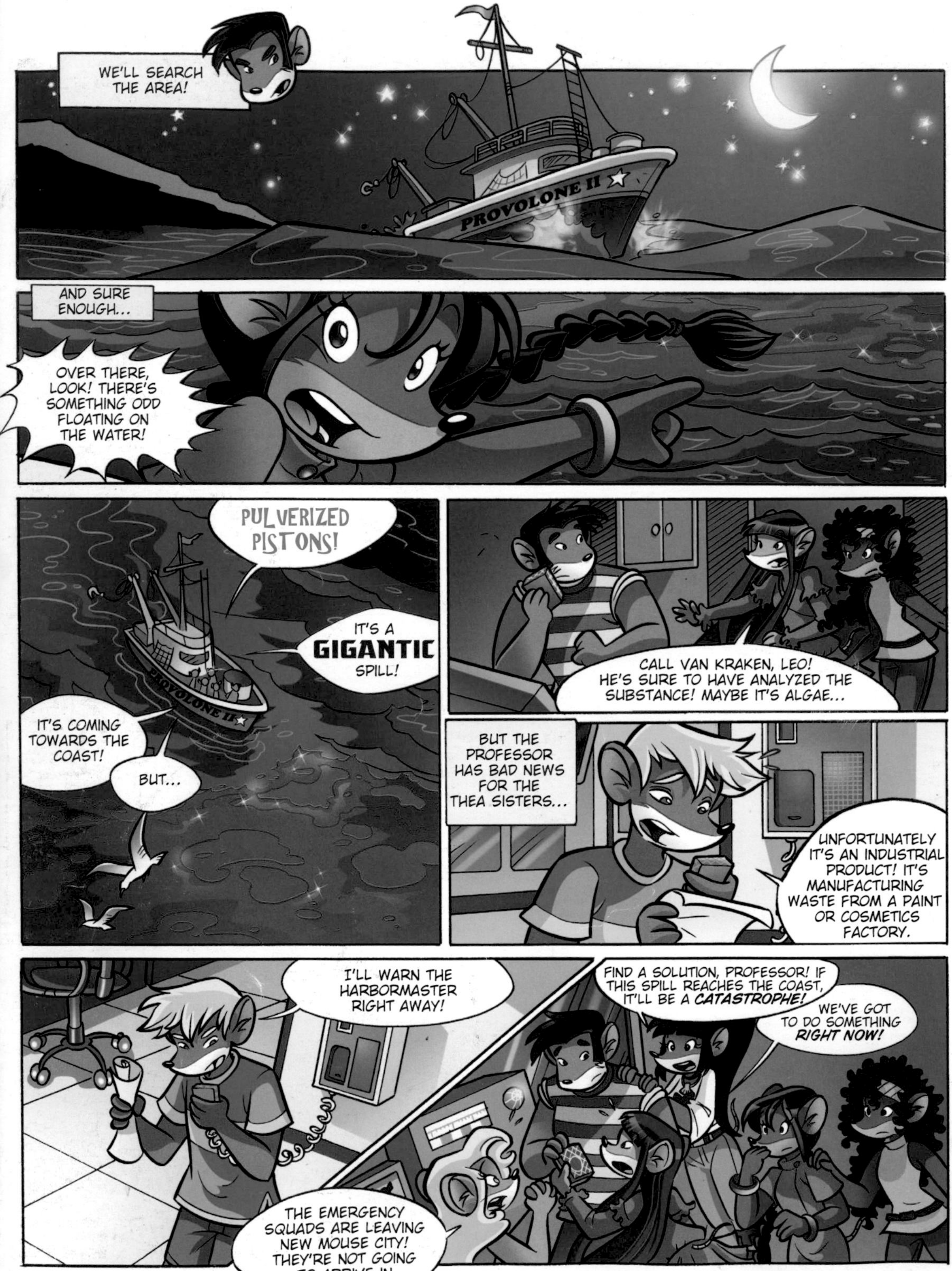
WE'LL SEARCH THE AREA!
PROVOLONE II
AND SURE ENOUGH...
OVER THERE, LOOK! THERE'S SOMETHING ODD FLOATING ON THE WATER!
PULVERIZED PISTONS!
IT'S A GIGANTIC SPILL!
IT'S COMING TOWARDS THE COAST!
BUT...
PROVOLONE II
CALL VAN KRAKEN, LEO! HE'S SURE TO HAVE ANALYZED THE SUBSTANCE! MAYBE IT'S ALGAE...
BUT THE PROFESSOR HAS BAD NEWS FOR THE THEA SISTERS...
UNFORTUNATELY IT'S AN INDUSTRIAL PRODUCT! IT'S MANUFACTURING WASTE FROM A PAINT OR COSMETICS FACTORY.
I'LL WARN THE HARBORMASTER RIGHT AWAY!
FIND A SOLUTION, PROFESSOR! IF THIS SPILL REACHES THE COAST, IT'LL BE A CATASTROPHE!
WE'VE GOT TO DO SOMETHING RIGHT NOW!
THE EMERGENCY SQUADS ARE LEAVING NEW MOUSE CITY! THEY'RE NOT GOING TO ARRIVE IN TIME!

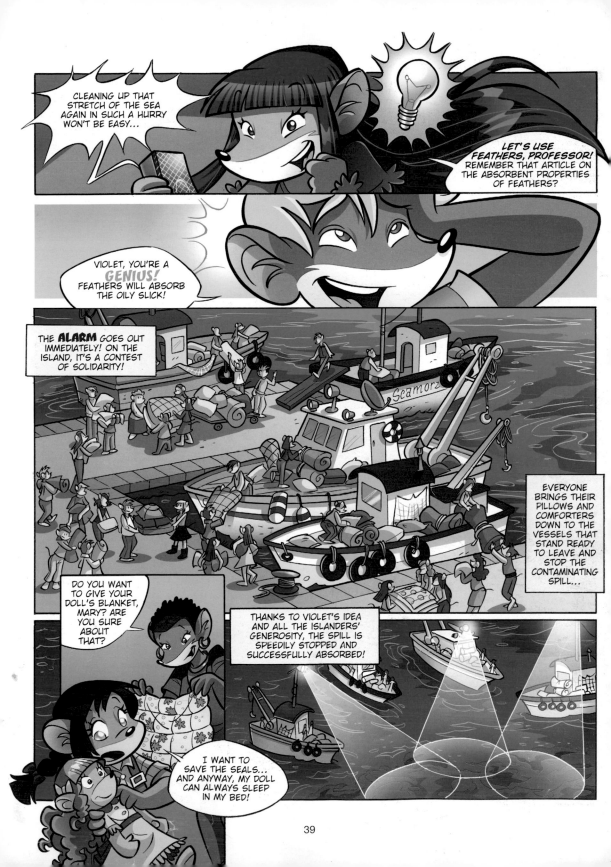

CLEANING UP THAT STRETCH OF THE SEA AGAIN IN SUCH A HURRY WON'T BE EASY...

LET'S USE FEATHERS, PROFESSOR! REMEMBER THAT ARTICLE ON THE ABSORBENT PROPERTIES OF FEATHERS?

VIOLET, YOU'RE A *GENIUS!* FEATHERS WILL ABSORB THE OILY SLICK!

THE **ALARM** GOES OUT IMMEDIATELY! ON THE ISLAND, IT'S A CONTEST OF SOLIDARITY!

EVERYONE BRINGS THEIR PILLOWS AND COMFORTERS DOWN TO THE VESSELS THAT STAND READY TO LEAVE AND STOP THE CONTAMINATING SPILL...

DO YOU WANT TO GIVE YOUR DOLL'S BLANKET, MARY? ARE YOU SURE ABOUT THAT?

THANKS TO VIOLET'S IDEA AND ALL THE ISLANDERS' GENEROSITY, THE SPILL IS SPEEDILY STOPPED AND SUCCESSFULLY ABSORBED!

I WANT TO SAVE THE SEALS... AND ANYWAY, MY DOLL CAN ALWAYS SLEEP IN MY BED!

39

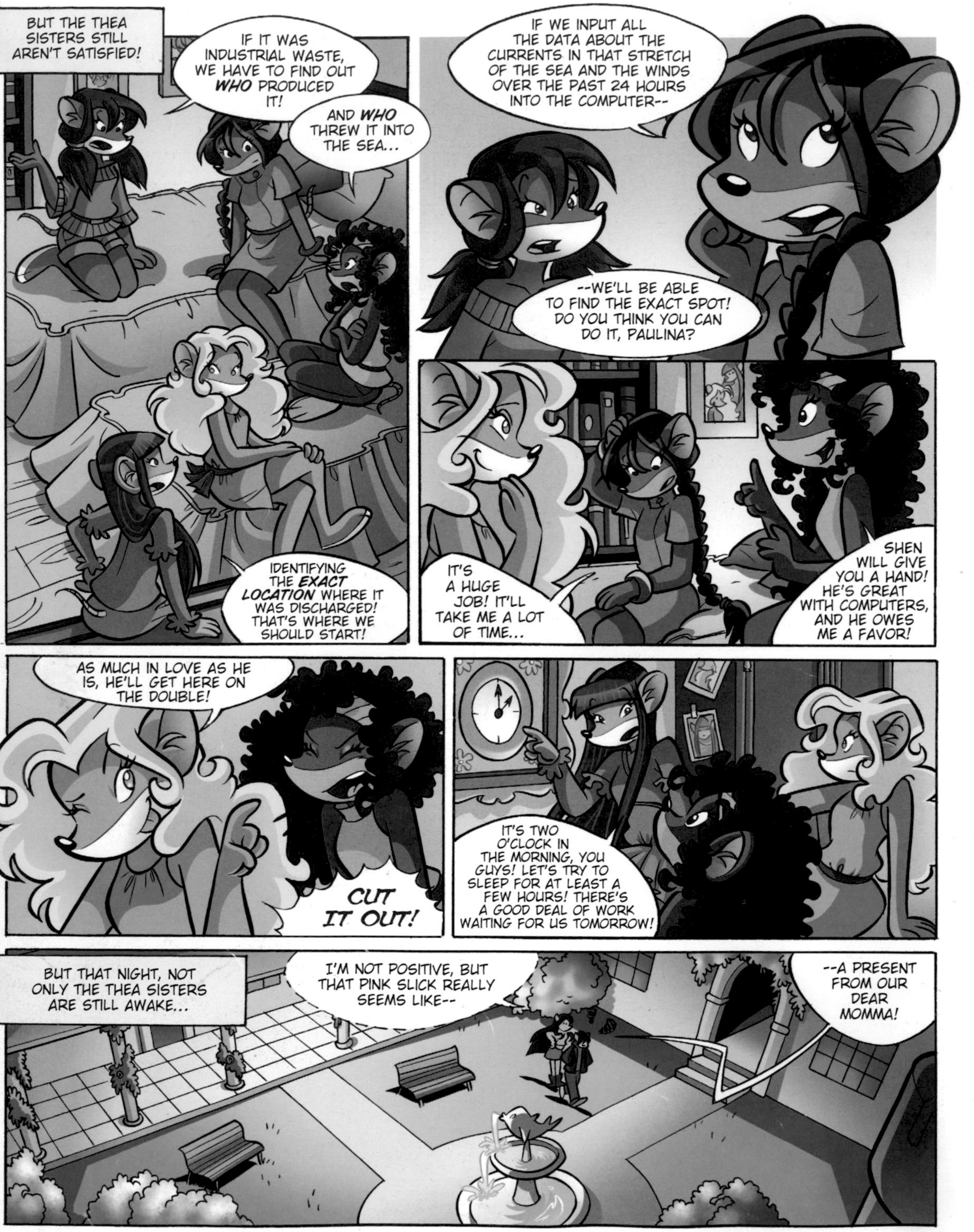
BUT THE THEA SISTERS STILL AREN'T SATISFIED!
IF IT WAS INDUSTRIAL WASTE, WE HAVE TO FIND OUT **WHO** PRODUCED IT!
AND **WHO** THREW IT INTO THE SEA...
IDENTIFYING THE **EXACT LOCATION** WHERE IT WAS DISCHARGED! THAT'S WHERE WE SHOULD START!
IF WE INPUT ALL THE DATA ABOUT THE CURRENTS IN THAT STRETCH OF THE SEA AND THE WINDS OVER THE PAST 24 HOURS INTO THE COMPUTER--
--WE'LL BE ABLE TO FIND THE EXACT SPOT! DO YOU THINK YOU CAN DO IT, PAULINA?
IT'S A HUGE JOB! IT'LL TAKE ME A LOT OF TIME...
SHEN WILL GIVE YOU A HAND! HE'S GREAT WITH COMPUTERS, AND HE OWES ME A FAVOR!
AS MUCH IN LOVE AS HE IS, HE'LL GET HERE ON THE DOUBLE!
CUT IT OUT!
IT'S TWO O'CLOCK IN THE MORNING, YOU GUYS! LET'S TRY TO SLEEP FOR AT LEAST A FEW HOURS! THERE'S A GOOD DEAL OF WORK WAITING FOR US TOMORROW!
BUT THAT NIGHT, NOT ONLY THE THEA SISTERS ARE STILL AWAKE...
I'M NOT POSITIVE, BUT THAT PINK SLICK REALLY SEEMS LIKE--
--A PRESENT FROM OUR DEAR MOMMA!

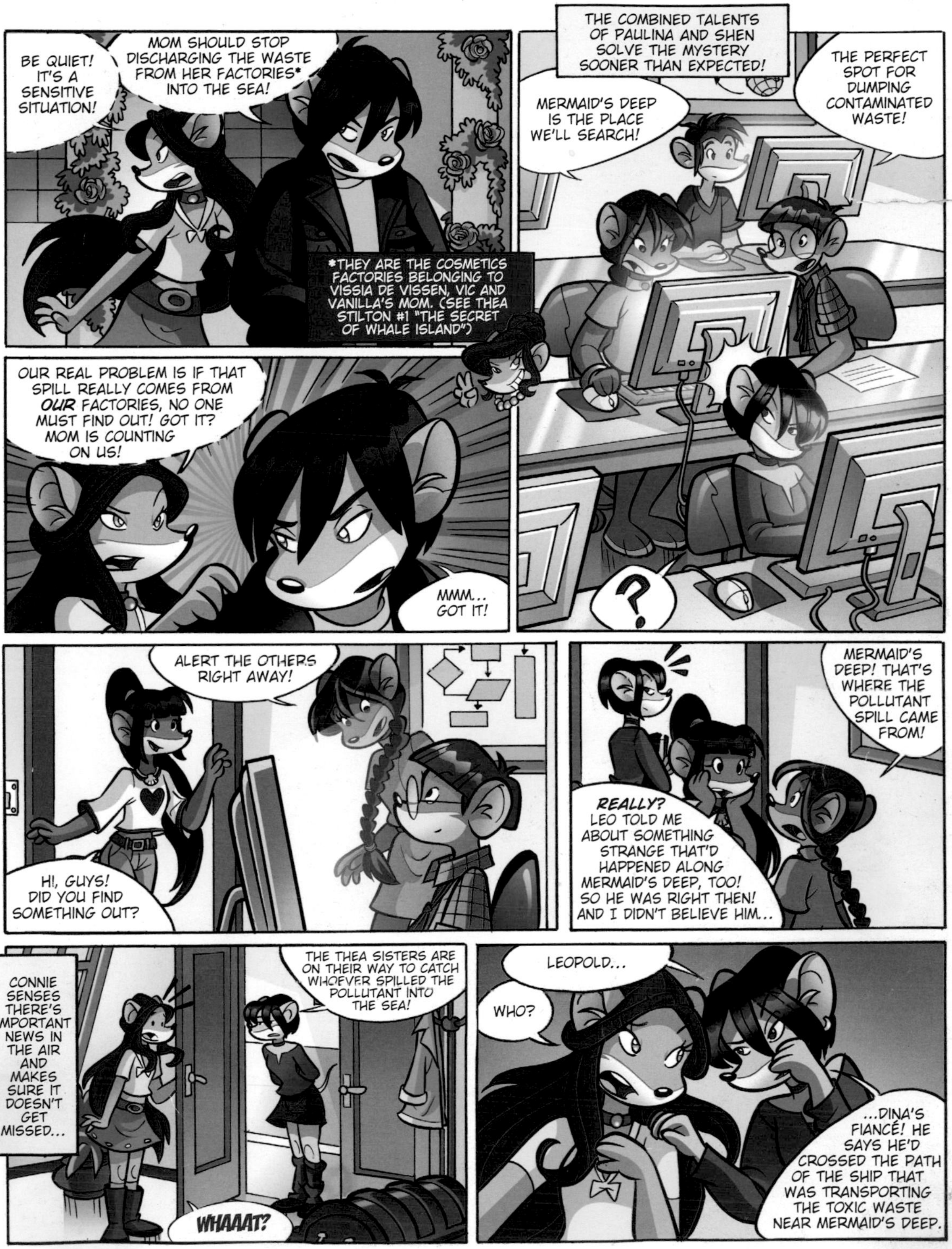
BE QUIET! IT'S A SENSITIVE SITUATION!
MOM SHOULD STOP DISCHARGING THE WASTE FROM HER FACTORIES* INTO THE SEA!
*THEY ARE THE COSMETICS FACTORIES BELONGING TO VISSIA DE VISSEN, VIC AND VANILLA'S MOM. (SEE THEA STILTON #1 "THE SECRET OF WHALE ISLAND")
THE COMBINED TALENTS OF PAULINA AND SHEN SOLVE THE MYSTERY SOONER THAN EXPECTED!
MERMAID'S DEEP IS THE PLACE WE'LL SEARCH!
THE PERFECT SPOT FOR DUMPING CONTAMINATED WASTE!
OUR REAL PROBLEM IS IF THAT SPILL REALLY COMES FROM OUR FACTORIES, NO ONE MUST FIND OUT! GOT IT? MOM IS COUNTING ON US!
MMM... GOT IT!
?
ALERT THE OTHERS RIGHT AWAY!
HI, GUYS! DID YOU FIND SOMETHING OUT?
MERMAID'S DEEP! THAT'S WHERE THE POLLUTANT SPILL CAME FROM!
REALLY? LEO TOLD ME ABOUT SOMETHING STRANGE THAT'D HAPPENED ALONG MERMAID'S DEEP, TOO! SO HE WAS RIGHT THEN! AND I DIDN'T BELIEVE HIM...
CONNIE SENSES THERE'S IMPORTANT NEWS IN THE AIR AND MAKES SURE IT DOESN'T GET MISSED...
THE THEA SISTERS ARE ON THEIR WAY TO CATCH WHOEVER SPILLED THE POLLUTANT INTO THE SEA!
WHAAAT?
LEOPOLD...
WHO?
...DINA'S FIANCÉ! HE SAYS HE'D CROSSED THE PATH OF THE SHIP THAT WAS TRANSPORTING THE TOXIC WASTE NEAR MERMAID'S DEEP.

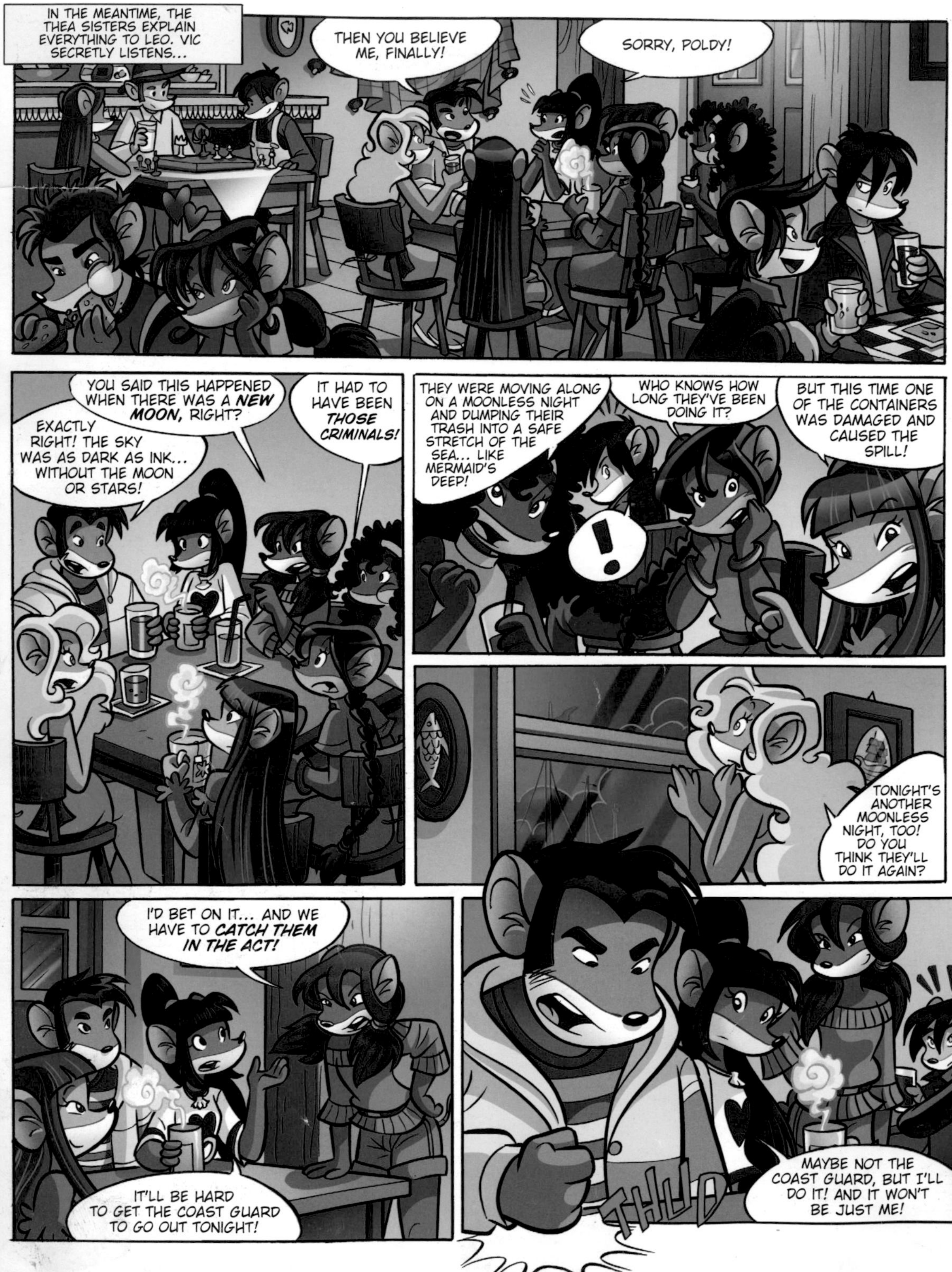
IN THE MEANTIME, THE THEA SISTERS EXPLAIN EVERYTHING TO LEO. VIC SECRETLY LISTENS...
THEN YOU BELIEVE ME, FINALLY!
SORRY, POLDY!
YOU SAID THIS HAPPENED WHEN THERE WAS A NEW MOON, RIGHT?
EXACTLY RIGHT! THE SKY WAS AS DARK AS INK... WITHOUT THE MOON OR STARS!
IT HAD TO HAVE BEEN THOSE CRIMINALS!
THEY WERE MOVING ALONG ON A MOONLESS NIGHT AND DUMPING THEIR TRASH INTO A SAFE STRETCH OF THE SEA... LIKE MERMAID'S DEEP!
WHO KNOWS HOW LONG THEY'VE BEEN DOING IT?
BUT THIS TIME ONE OF THE CONTAINERS WAS DAMAGED AND CAUSED THE SPILL!
!
TONIGHT'S ANOTHER MOONLESS NIGHT, TOO! DO YOU THINK THEY'LL DO IT AGAIN?
I'D BET ON IT... AND WE HAVE TO CATCH THEM IN THE ACT!
IT'LL BE HARD TO GET THE COAST GUARD TO GO OUT TONIGHT!
THUD
MAYBE NOT THE COAST GUARD, BUT I'LL DO IT! AND IT WON'T BE JUST ME!

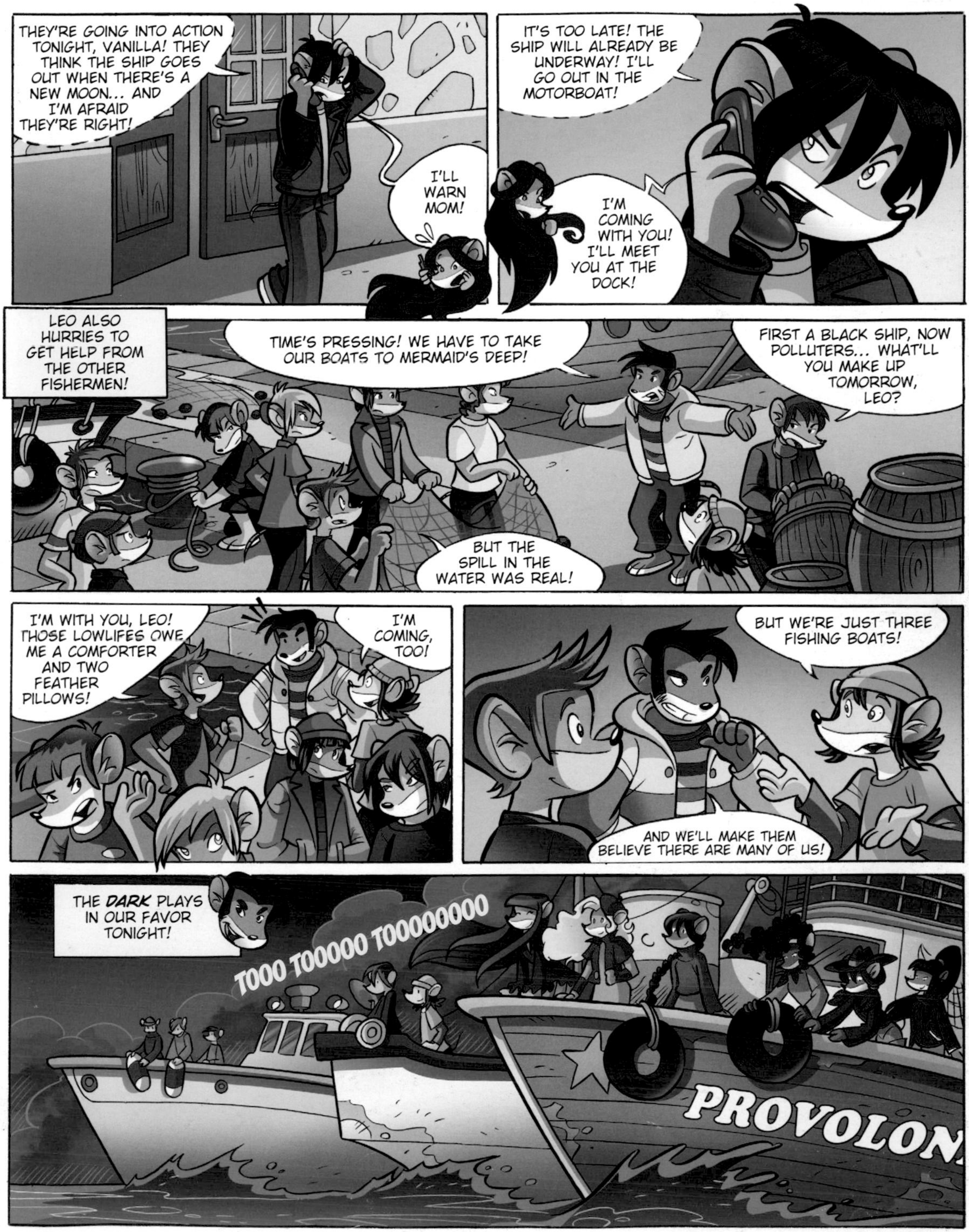

THEY'RE GOING INTO ACTION TONIGHT, VANILLA! THEY THINK THE SHIP GOES OUT WHEN THERE'S A NEW MOON... AND I'M AFRAID THEY'RE RIGHT!
I'LL WARN MOM!
IT'S TOO LATE! THE SHIP WILL ALREADY BE UNDERWAY! I'LL GO OUT IN THE MOTORBOAT!
I'M COMING WITH YOU! I'LL MEET YOU AT THE DOCK!
LEO ALSO HURRIES TO GET HELP FROM THE OTHER FISHERMEN!
TIME'S PRESSING! WE HAVE TO TAKE OUR BOATS TO MERMAID'S DEEP!
FIRST A BLACK SHIP, NOW POLLUTERS... WHAT'LL YOU MAKE UP TOMORROW, LEO?
BUT THE SPILL IN THE WATER WAS REAL!
I'M WITH YOU, LEO! THOSE LOWLIFES OWE ME A COMFORTER AND TWO FEATHER PILLOWS!
I'M COMING, TOO!
BUT WE'RE JUST THREE FISHING BOATS!
AND WE'LL MAKE THEM BELIEVE THERE ARE MANY OF US!
THE DARK PLAYS IN OUR FAVOR TONIGHT!
TOOO TOOOOO TOOOOOOOO
PROVOLON

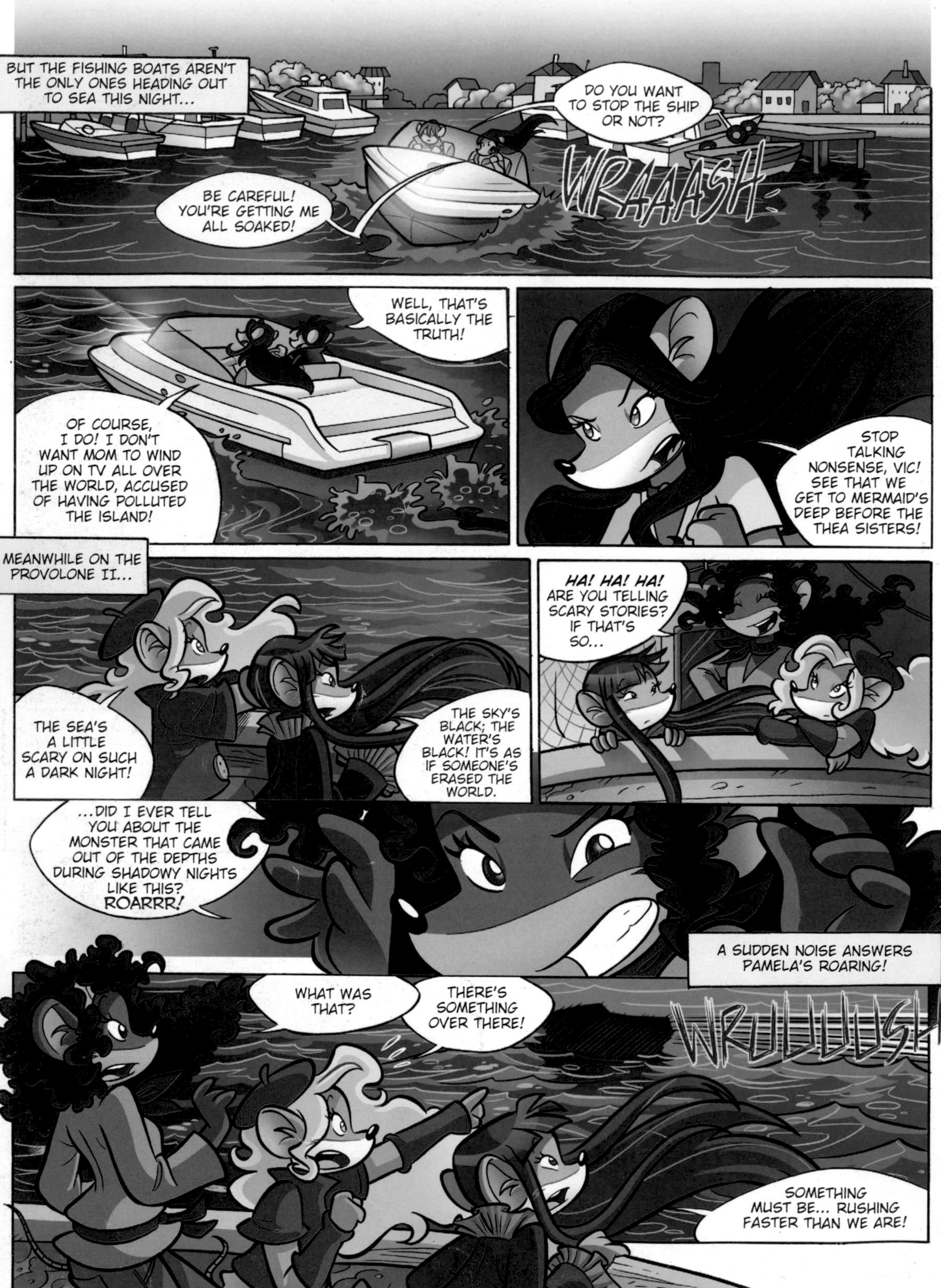

BUT THE FISHING BOATS AREN'T THE ONLY ONES HEADING OUT TO SEA THIS NIGHT...
DO YOU WANT TO STOP THE SHIP OR NOT?
WRAAASH
BE CAREFUL! YOU'RE GETTING ME ALL SOAKED!
WELL, THAT'S BASICALLY THE TRUTH!
OF COURSE, I DO! I DON'T WANT MOM TO WIND UP ON TV ALL OVER THE WORLD, ACCUSED OF HAVING POLLUTED THE ISLAND!
STOP TALKING NONSENSE, VIC! SEE THAT WE GET TO MERMAID'S DEEP BEFORE THE THEA SISTERS!
MEANWHILE ON THE PROVOLONE II...
THE SEA'S A LITTLE SCARY ON SUCH A DARK NIGHT!
THE SKY'S BLACK; THE WATER'S BLACK! IT'S AS IF SOMEONE'S ERASED THE WORLD.
HA! HA! HA! ARE YOU TELLING SCARY STORIES? IF THAT'S SO...
...DID I EVER TELL YOU ABOUT THE MONSTER THAT CAME OUT OF THE DEPTHS DURING SHADOWY NIGHTS LIKE THIS? ROARRR!
A SUDDEN NOISE ANSWERS PAMELA'S ROARING!
WHAT WAS THAT?
THERE'S SOMETHING OVER THERE!
WRUUUUSH
SOMETHING MUST BE... RUSHING FASTER THAN WE ARE!

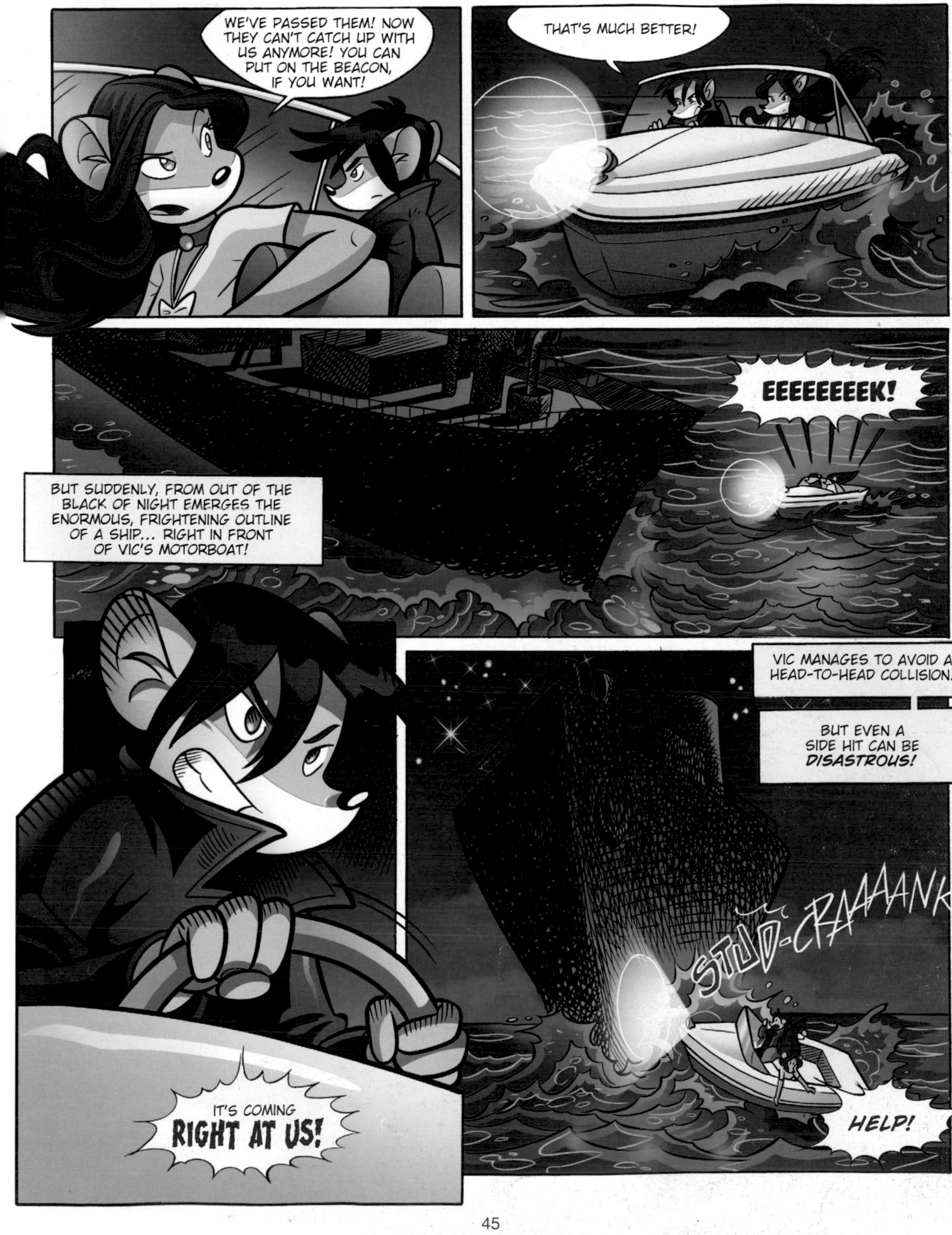
WE'VE PASSED THEM! NOW THEY CAN'T CATCH UP WITH US ANYMORE! YOU CAN PUT ON THE BEACON, IF YOU WANT!
THAT'S MUCH BETTER!
EEEEEEEEK!
BUT SUDDENLY, FROM OUT OF THE BLACK OF NIGHT EMERGES THE ENORMOUS, FRIGHTENING OUTLINE OF A SHIP... RIGHT IN FRONT OF VIC'S MOTORBOAT!
IT'S COMING RIGHT AT US!
VIC MANAGES TO AVOID A HEAD-TO-HEAD COLLISION!
BUT EVEN A SIDE HIT CAN BE DISASTROUS!
STUD-CRAAAANK
HELP!

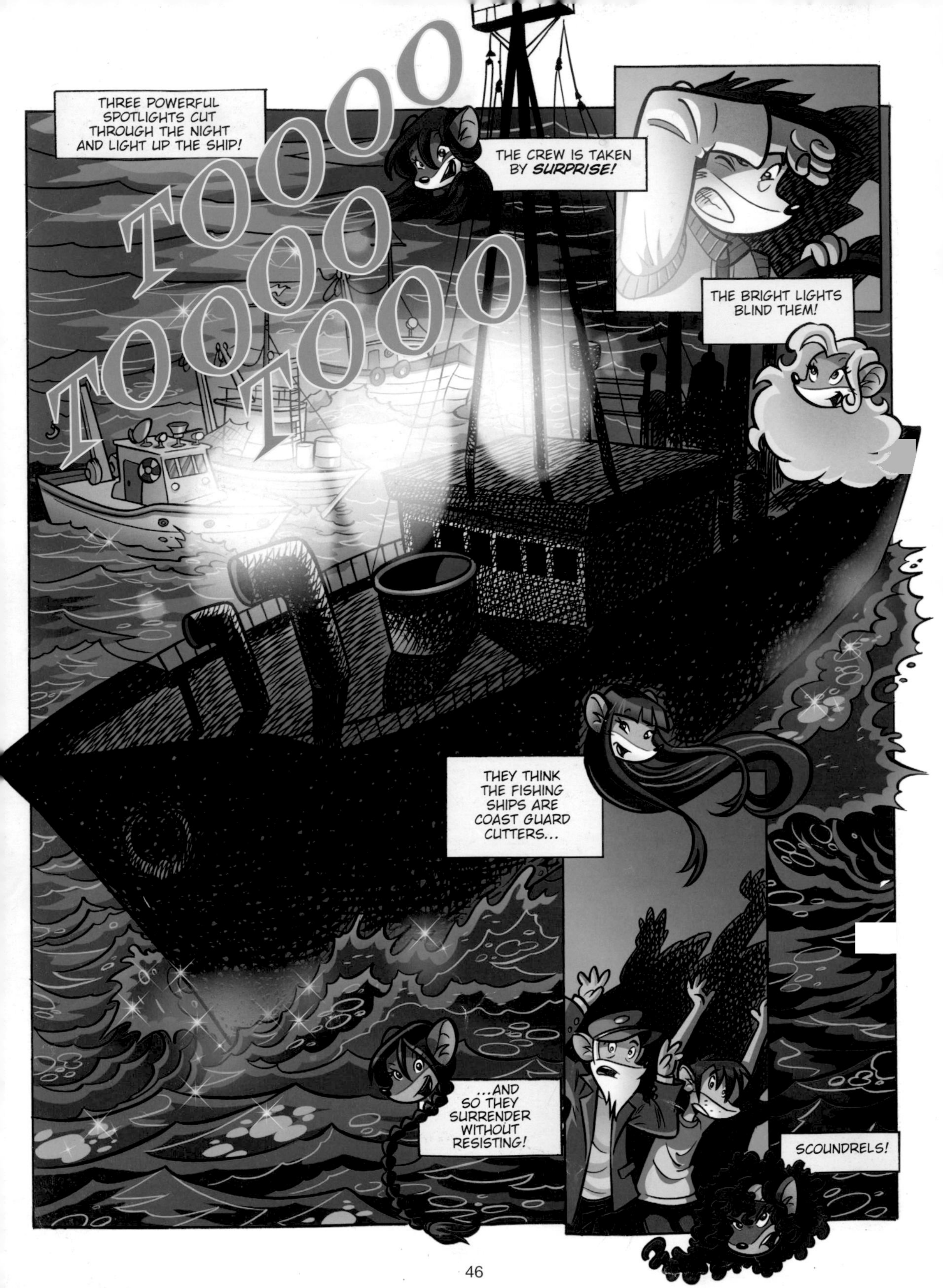

THREE POWERFUL SPOTLIGHTS CUT THROUGH THE NIGHT AND LIGHT UP THE SHIP!
TOOOOO TOOOO TOOOO
THE CREW IS TAKEN BY SURPRISE!
THE BRIGHT LIGHTS BLIND THEM!
THEY THINK THE FISHING SHIPS ARE COAST GUARD CUTTERS...
...AND SO THEY SURRENDER WITHOUT RESISTING!
SCOUNDRELS!

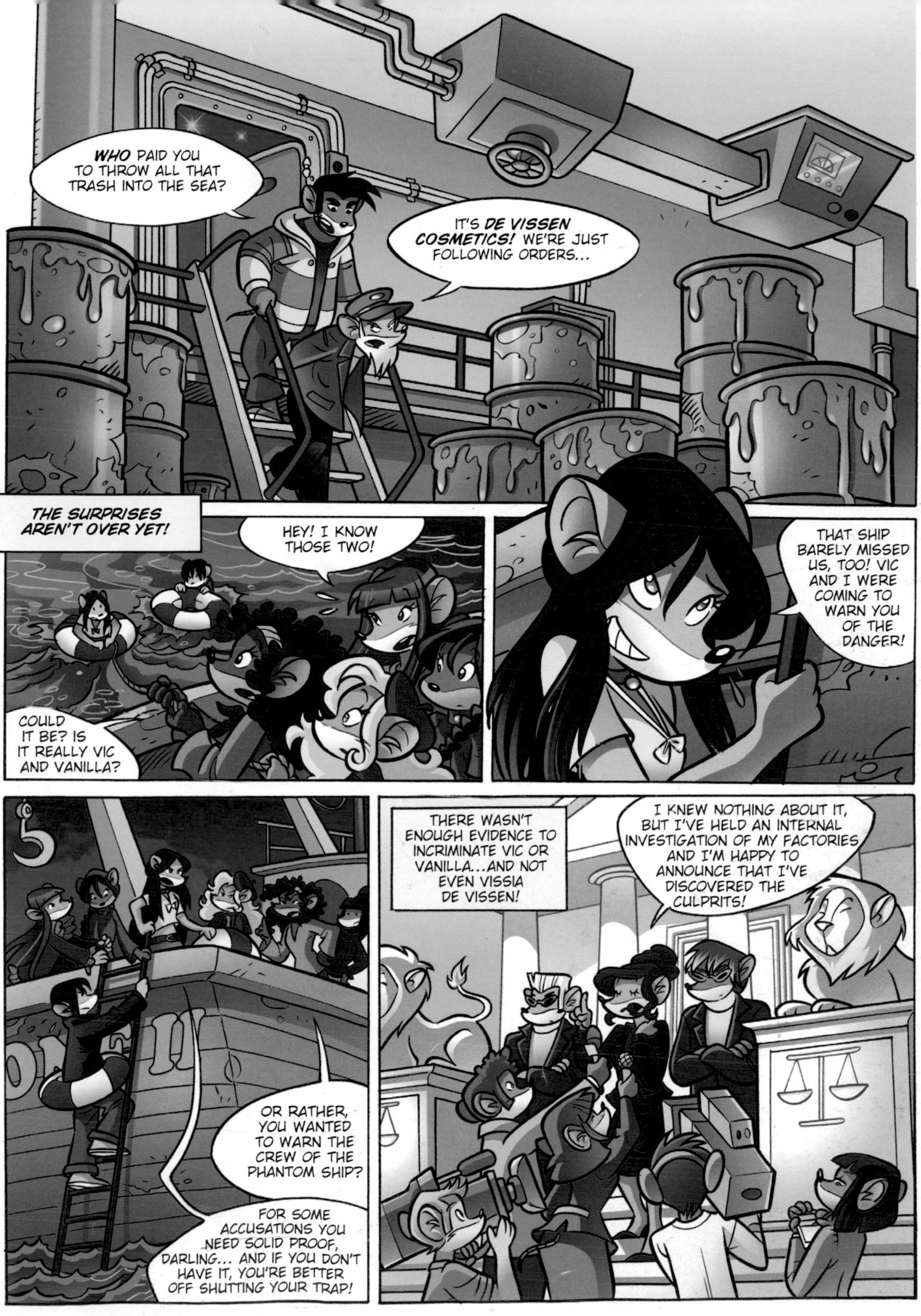

WHO PAID YOU TO THROW ALL THAT TRASH INTO THE SEA?
IT'S **DE VISSEN COSMETICS!** WE'RE JUST FOLLOWING ORDERS...
THE SURPRISES AREN'T OVER YET!
HEY! I KNOW THOSE TWO!
COULD IT BE? IS IT REALLY VIC AND VANILLA?
THAT SHIP BARELY MISSED US, TOO! VIC AND I WERE COMING TO WARN YOU OF THE DANGER!
OR RATHER, YOU WANTED TO WARN THE CREW OF THE PHANTOM SHIP?
FOR SOME ACCUSATIONS YOU NEED SOLID PROOF, DARLING... AND IF YOU DON'T HAVE IT, YOU'RE BETTER OFF SHUTTING YOUR TRAP!
THERE WASN'T ENOUGH EVIDENCE TO INCRIMINATE VIC OR VANILLA...AND NOT EVEN VISSIA DE VISSEN!
I KNEW NOTHING ABOUT IT, BUT I'VE HELD AN INTERNAL INVESTIGATION OF MY FACTORIES AND I'M HAPPY TO ANNOUNCE THAT I'VE DISCOVERED THE CULPRITS!

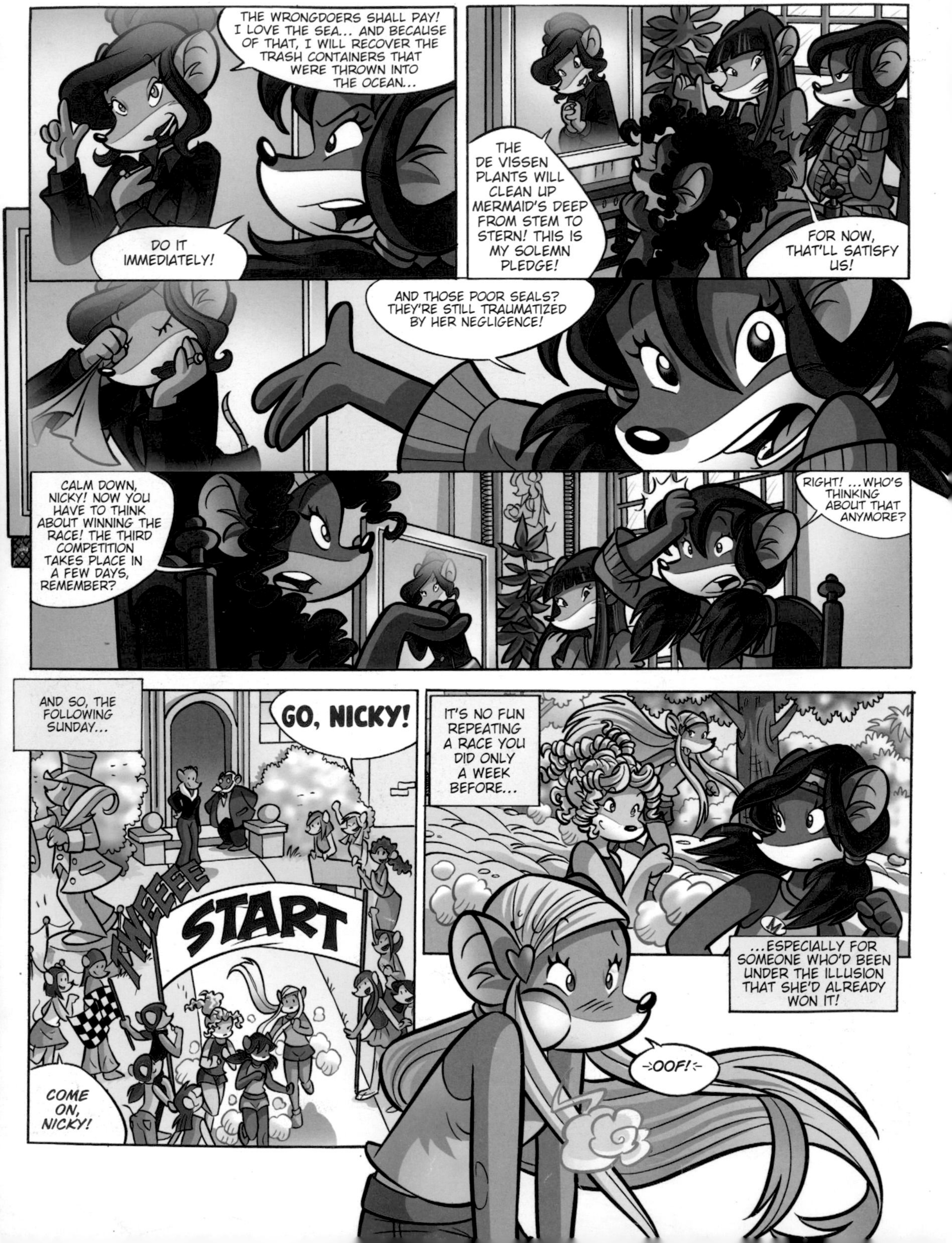

THE WRONGDOERS SHALL PAY! I LOVE THE SEA... AND BECAUSE OF THAT, I WILL RECOVER THE TRASH CONTAINERS THAT WERE THROWN INTO THE OCEAN...
DO IT IMMEDIATELY!
THE DE VISSEN PLANTS WILL CLEAN UP MERMAID'S DEEP FROM STEM TO STERN! THIS IS MY SOLEMN PLEDGE!
FOR NOW, THAT'LL SATISFY US!
AND THOSE POOR SEALS? THEY'RE STILL TRAUMATIZED BY HER NEGLIGENCE!
CALM DOWN, NICKY! NOW YOU HAVE TO THINK ABOUT WINNING THE RACE! THE THIRD COMPETITION TAKES PLACE IN A FEW DAYS, REMEMBER?
RIGHT! ...WHO'S THINKING ABOUT THAT ANYMORE?
AND SO, THE FOLLOWING SUNDAY...
GO, NICKY!
TWEEEE
START
COME ON, NICKY!
IT'S NO FUN REPEATING A RACE YOU DID ONLY A WEEK BEFORE...
...ESPECIALLY FOR SOMEONE WHO'D BEEN UNDER THE ILLUSION THAT SHE'D ALREADY WON IT!
OOF!

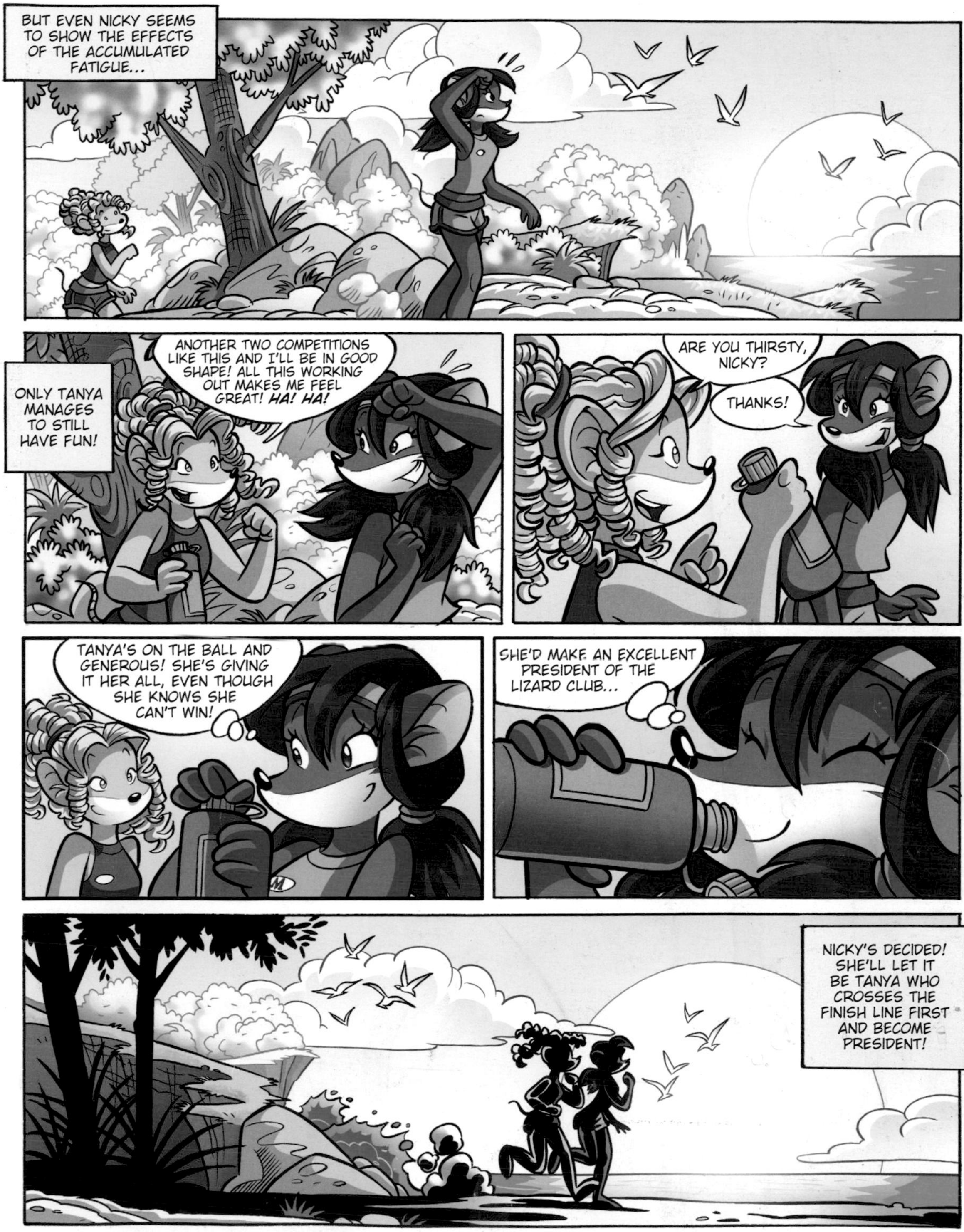
BUT EVEN NICKY SEEMS TO SHOW THE EFFECTS OF THE ACCUMULATED FATIGUE...
ONLY TANYA MANAGES TO STILL HAVE FUN!
ANOTHER TWO COMPETITIONS LIKE THIS AND I'LL BE IN GOOD SHAPE! ALL THIS WORKING OUT MAKES ME FEEL GREAT! HA! HA!
ARE YOU THIRSTY, NICKY?
THANKS!
TANYA'S ON THE BALL AND GENEROUS! SHE'S GIVING IT HER ALL, EVEN THOUGH SHE KNOWS SHE CAN'T WIN!
SHE'D MAKE AN EXCELLENT PRESIDENT OF THE LIZARD CLUB...
NICKY'S DECIDED! SHE'LL LET IT BE TANYA WHO CROSSES THE FINISH LINE FIRST AND BECOME PRESIDENT!

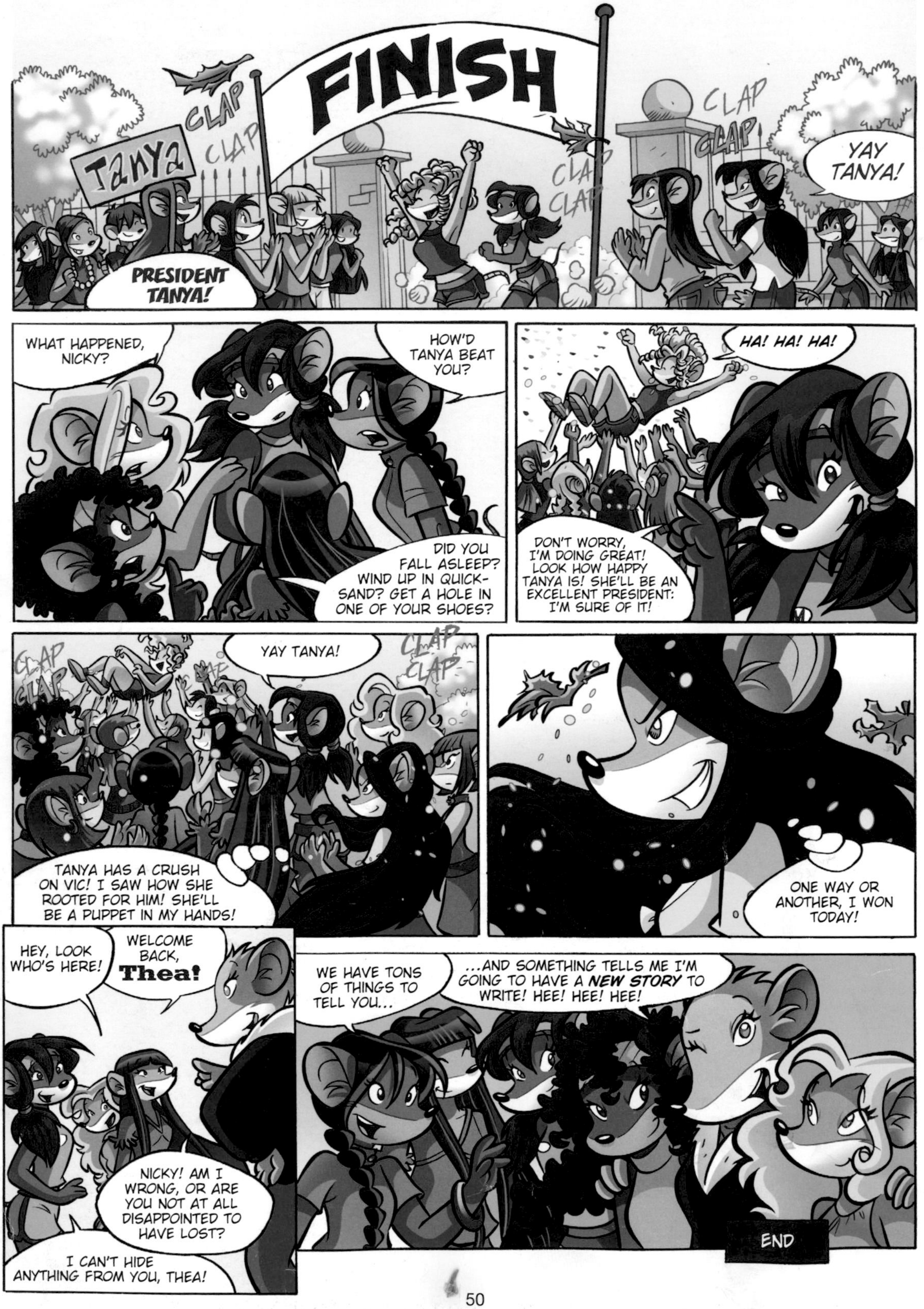
FINISH
CLAP
CLAP
Tanya
CLAP
CLAP
CLAP
CLAP
YAY TANYA!
PRESIDENT TANYA!
WHAT HAPPENED, NICKY?
HOW'D TANYA BEAT YOU?
DID YOU FALL ASLEEP? WIND UP IN QUICK-SAND? GET A HOLE IN ONE OF YOUR SHOES?
HA! HA! HA!
DON'T WORRY, I'M DOING GREAT! LOOK HOW HAPPY TANYA IS! SHE'LL BE AN EXCELLENT PRESIDENT: I'M SURE OF IT!
CLAP
CLAP
YAY TANYA!
CLAP
CLAP
TANYA HAS A CRUSH ON VIC! I SAW HOW SHE ROOTED FOR HIM! SHE'LL BE A PUPPET IN MY HANDS!
ONE WAY OR ANOTHER, I WON TODAY!
HEY, LOOK WHO'S HERE!
WELCOME BACK, Thea!
NICKY! AM I WRONG, OR ARE YOU NOT AT ALL DISAPPOINTED TO HAVE LOST?
I CAN'T HIDE ANYTHING FROM YOU, THEA!
WE HAVE TONS OF THINGS TO TELL YOU...
...AND SOMETHING TELLS ME I'M GOING TO HAVE A NEW STORY TO WRITE! HEE! HEE! HEE!
END

Watch Out For PAPERCUTZ™

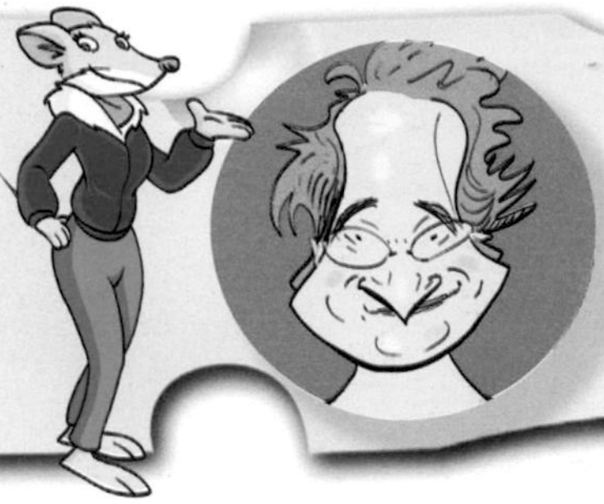

I'm tempted to dress up in a white suit and say to you "Welcome to Fantasy Island," but I'm sure that won't mean anything to you. You see, years and years ago, there was a popular TV show about this magical place that you could travel to, and once there, your dreams would come true. In some ways, Whale Island is very similar. Instead of travelers, students such as Colette, Violet, Pamela, Nicky, and Paulina have come to Whale Island to attend Mouseford Academy to work hard as students to help make their dreams come true!

Oh, I almost forgot to introduce myself! I'm Salicrup, *Jim Salicrup,* the Editor-in-Chief of Papercutz, the cheese-loving folks dedicated to publishing great graphic novels for all ages. I'm here to welcome you to the sophomore THEA STILTON graphic novel. If you've never seen a THEA STILTON graphic novel before, we sincerely hope you really enjoy it! While it may be a little confusing to call the series "THEA STILTON," we believe once you get to know the Thea Sisters, you'll understand that Thea serves as the inspiration to these wonderful girls, and that her adventurous spirit is felt on every page! If you've already seen THEA STILTON #1 "The Secret of Whale Island," then welcome back! And if you've also been collecting the Papercutz GERONIMO STILTON graphic novels, well, I could just hug you!

But as thrilled as I am that you're enjoying our THEA STILTON and GERONIMO STILTON graphic novels, I'd also like you to be aware of the many other graphic novel series also published by your pals at Papercutz! From such world-famous characters as Garfield, The Smurfs, Tinker Bell, and Nancy Drew to such exciting new characters as Ernest & Rebecca, Sybil the Backpack Fairy, Benny Breakiron, and ARiOL we're publishing a wide array of comics designed to entertain you! If you haven't yet visited the Papercutz website, may I suggest checking it out at your soonest opportunity? I just know you'll find a graphic novel or two to fall in love with!

But no matter what, be sure not to miss THEA STILTON #3 "The Treasure of the Viking Ship," coming soon! There's even a special preview on the very next page!

Class dismissed!

JiM

Stay in Touch!

EMAIL:	salicrup@papercutz.com
WEB:	www.papercutz.com
TWITTER:	@papercutzgn
FACEBOOK:	PAPERCUTZGRAPHICNOVELS
FAN MAIL:	Papercutz, 160 Broadway, Suite 700, East Wing, New York, NY 10038

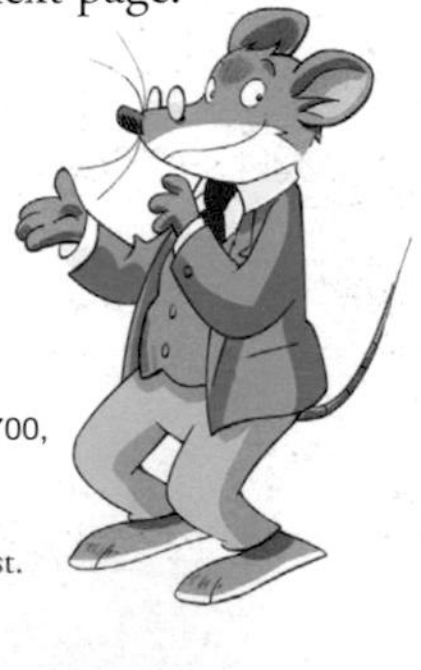

Caricature of Jim by Steve Brodner at the MoCCA Art Fest.

Special Preview of THEA STILTON #3 "The Treasure of the Viking Ship!"

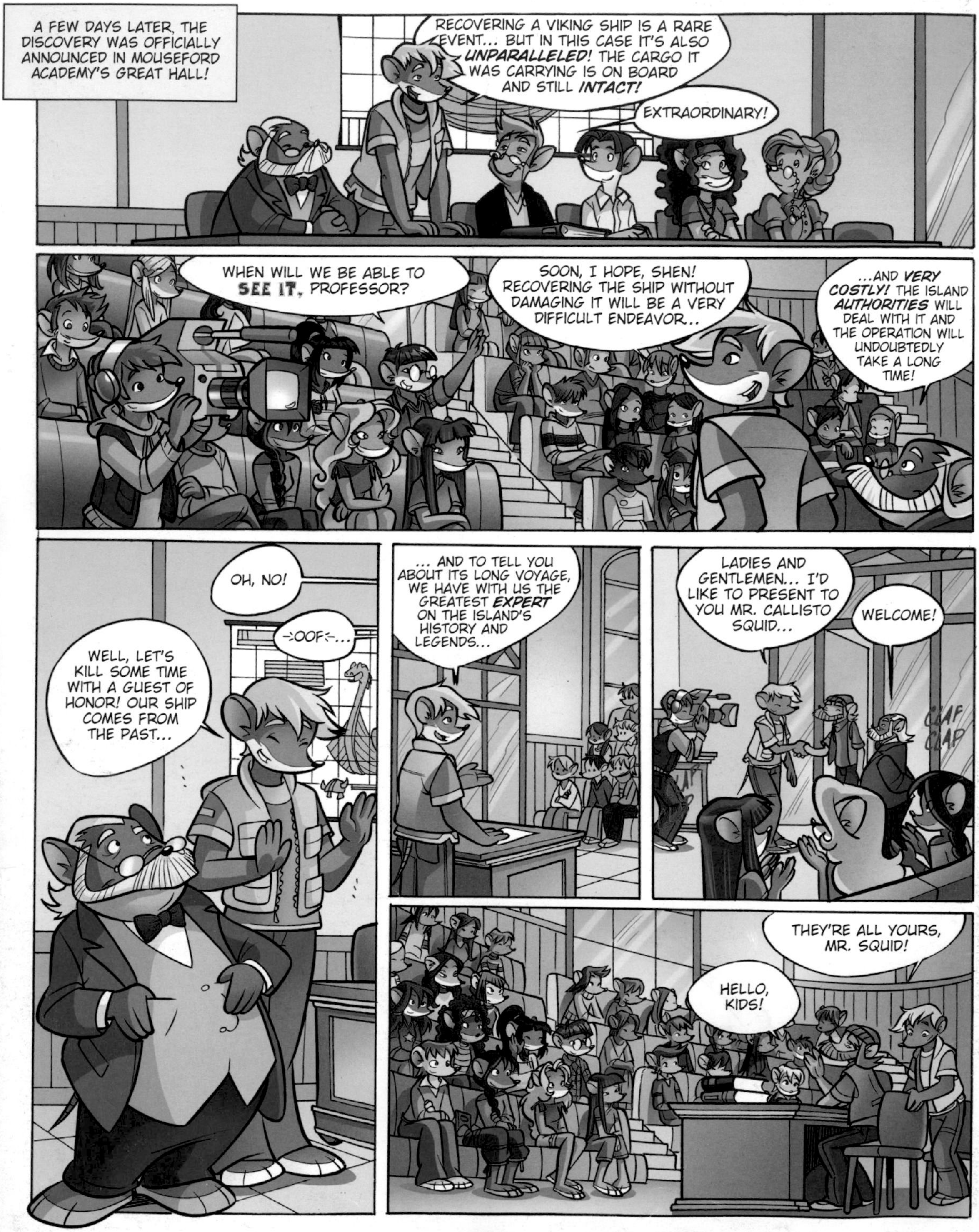
A FEW DAYS LATER, THE DISCOVERY WAS OFFICIALLY ANNOUNCED IN MOUSEFORD ACADEMY'S GREAT HALL!
RECOVERING A VIKING SHIP IS A RARE EVENT... BUT IN THIS CASE IT'S ALSO UNPARALLELED! THE CARGO IT WAS CARRYING IS ON BOARD AND STILL INTACT!
EXTRAORDINARY!
WHEN WILL WE BE ABLE TO SEE IT, PROFESSOR?
SOON, I HOPE, SHEN! RECOVERING THE SHIP WITHOUT DAMAGING IT WILL BE A VERY DIFFICULT ENDEAVOR...
...AND VERY COSTLY! THE ISLAND AUTHORITIES WILL DEAL WITH IT AND THE OPERATION WILL UNDOUBTEDLY TAKE A LONG TIME!
OH, NO!
-OOF-...
WELL, LET'S KILL SOME TIME WITH A GUEST OF HONOR! OUR SHIP COMES FROM THE PAST...
... AND TO TELL YOU ABOUT ITS LONG VOYAGE, WE HAVE WITH US THE GREATEST EXPERT ON THE ISLAND'S HISTORY AND LEGENDS...
LADIES AND GENTLEMEN... I'D LIKE TO PRESENT TO YOU MR. CALLISTO SQUID...
WELCOME!
CLAP CLAP
THEY'RE ALL YOURS, MR. SQUID!
HELLO, KIDS!

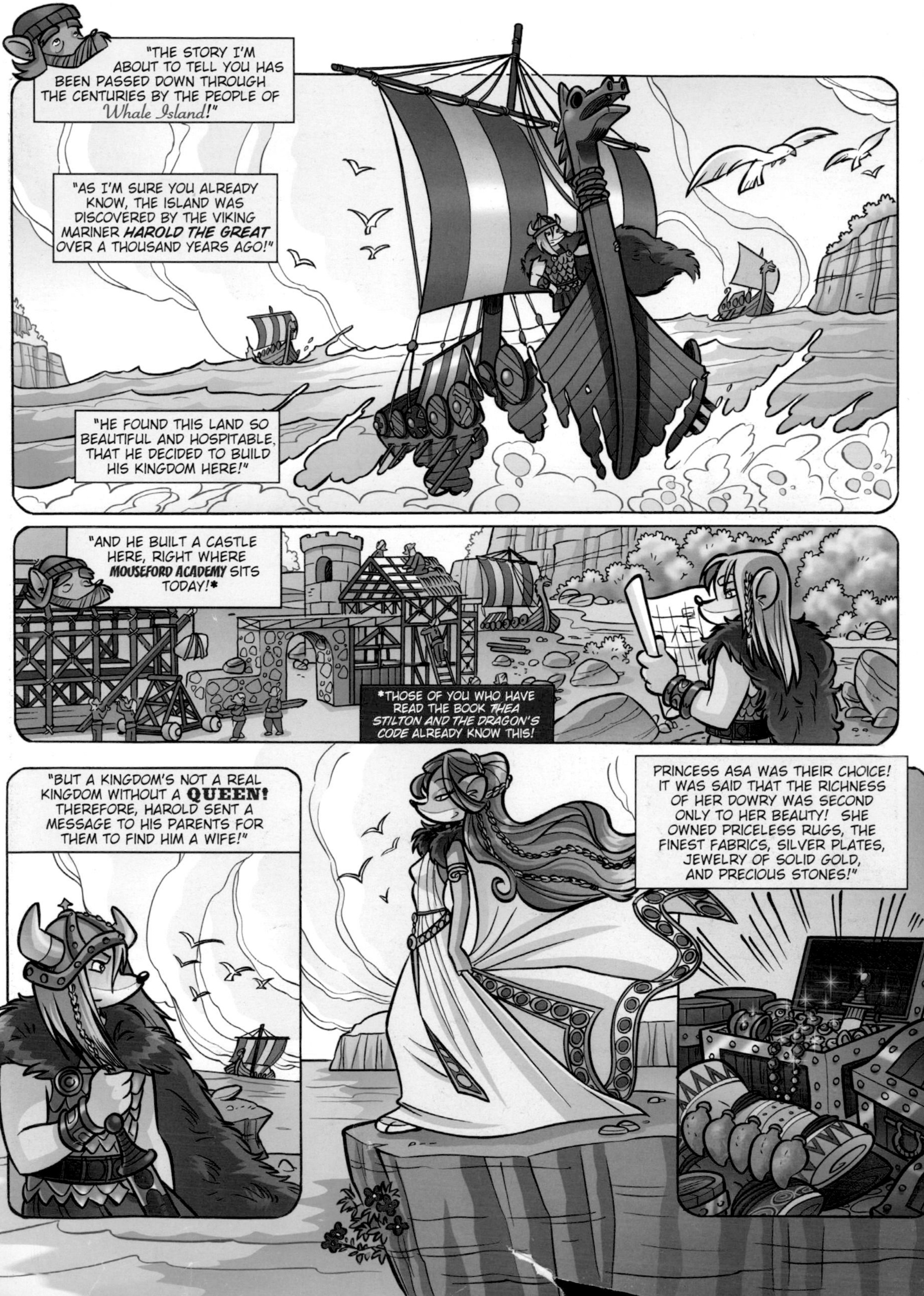
"THE STORY I'M ABOUT TO TELL YOU HAS BEEN PASSED DOWN THROUGH THE CENTURIES BY THE PEOPLE OF Whale Island!"
"AS I'M SURE YOU ALREADY KNOW, THE ISLAND WAS DISCOVERED BY THE VIKING MARINER HAROLD THE GREAT OVER A THOUSAND YEARS AGO!"
"HE FOUND THIS LAND SO BEAUTIFUL AND HOSPITABLE, THAT HE DECIDED TO BUILD HIS KINGDOM HERE!"
"AND HE BUILT A CASTLE HERE, RIGHT WHERE MOUSEFORD ACADEMY SITS TODAY!*
*THOSE OF YOU WHO HAVE READ THE BOOK THEA STILTON AND THE DRAGON'S CODE ALREADY KNOW THIS!
"BUT A KINGDOM'S NOT A REAL KINGDOM WITHOUT A QUEEN! THEREFORE, HAROLD SENT A MESSAGE TO HIS PARENTS FOR THEM TO FIND HIM A WIFE!"
PRINCESS ASA WAS THEIR CHOICE! IT WAS SAID THAT THE RICHNESS OF HER DOWRY WAS SECOND ONLY TO HER BEAUTY! SHE OWNED PRICELESS RUGS, THE FINEST FABRICS, SILVER PLATES, JEWELRY OF SOLID GOLD, AND PRECIOUS STONES!"

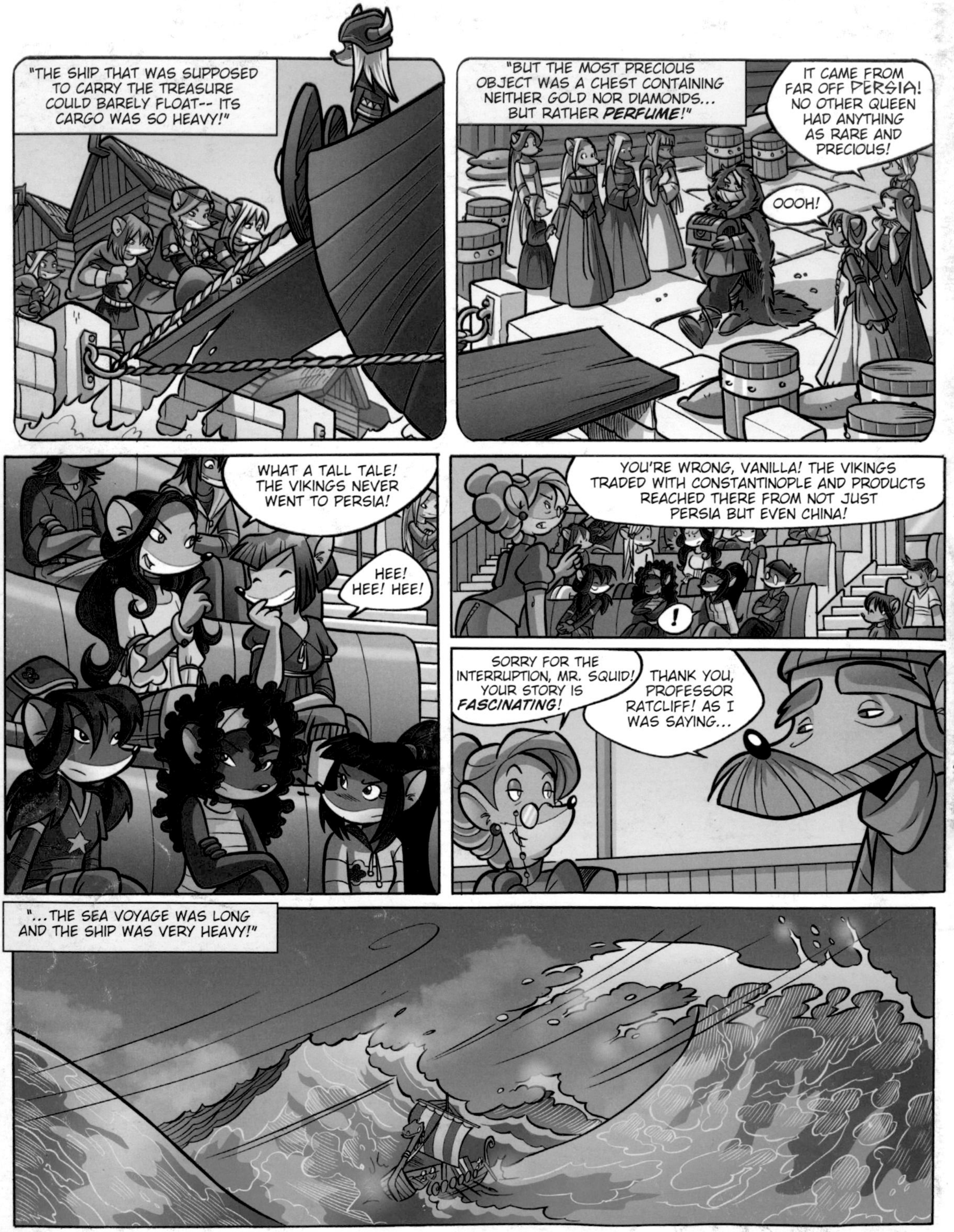
"THE SHIP THAT WAS SUPPOSED TO CARRY THE TREASURE COULD BARELY FLOAT-- ITS CARGO WAS SO HEAVY!"
"BUT THE MOST PRECIOUS OBJECT WAS A CHEST CONTAINING NEITHER GOLD NOR DIAMONDS... BUT RATHER PERFUME!"
IT CAME FROM FAR OFF PERSIA! NO OTHER QUEEN HAD ANYTHING AS RARE AND PRECIOUS!
OOOH!
WHAT A TALL TALE! THE VIKINGS NEVER WENT TO PERSIA!
HEE! HEE! HEE!
YOU'RE WRONG, VANILLA! THE VIKINGS TRADED WITH CONSTANTINOPLE AND PRODUCTS REACHED THERE FROM NOT JUST PERSIA BUT EVEN CHINA!
!
SORRY FOR THE INTERRUPTION, MR. SQUID! YOUR STORY IS FASCINATING!
THANK YOU, PROFESSOR RATCLIFF! AS I WAS SAYING...
"...THE SEA VOYAGE WAS LONG AND THE SHIP WAS VERY HEAVY!"

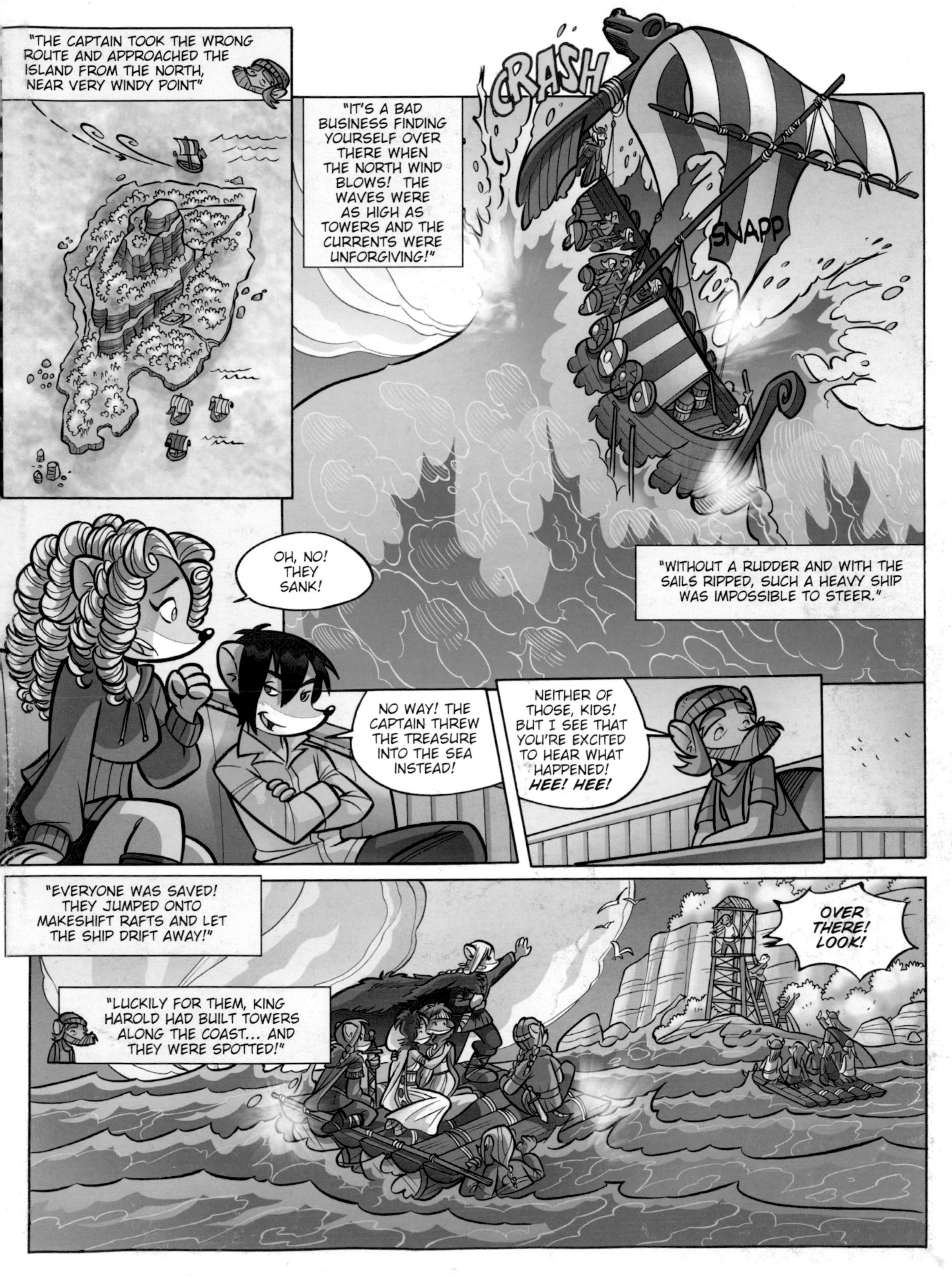
"THE CAPTAIN TOOK THE WRONG ROUTE AND APPROACHED THE ISLAND FROM THE NORTH, NEAR VERY WINDY POINT"
"IT'S A BAD BUSINESS FINDING YOURSELF OVER THERE WHEN THE NORTH WIND BLOWS! THE WAVES WERE AS HIGH AS TOWERS AND THE CURRENTS WERE UNFORGIVING!"
CRASH
SNAPP
"WITHOUT A RUDDER AND WITH THE SAILS RIPPED, SUCH A HEAVY SHIP WAS IMPOSSIBLE TO STEER."
OH, NO! THEY SANK!
NO WAY! THE CAPTAIN THREW THE TREASURE INTO THE SEA INSTEAD!
NEITHER OF THOSE, KIDS! BUT I SEE THAT YOU'RE EXCITED TO HEAR WHAT HAPPENED! HEE! HEE!
"EVERYONE WAS SAVED! THEY JUMPED ONTO MAKESHIFT RAFTS AND LET THE SHIP DRIFT AWAY!"
"LUCKILY FOR THEM, KING HAROLD HAD BUILT TOWERS ALONG THE COAST... AND THEY WERE SPOTTED!"
OVER THERE! LOOK!

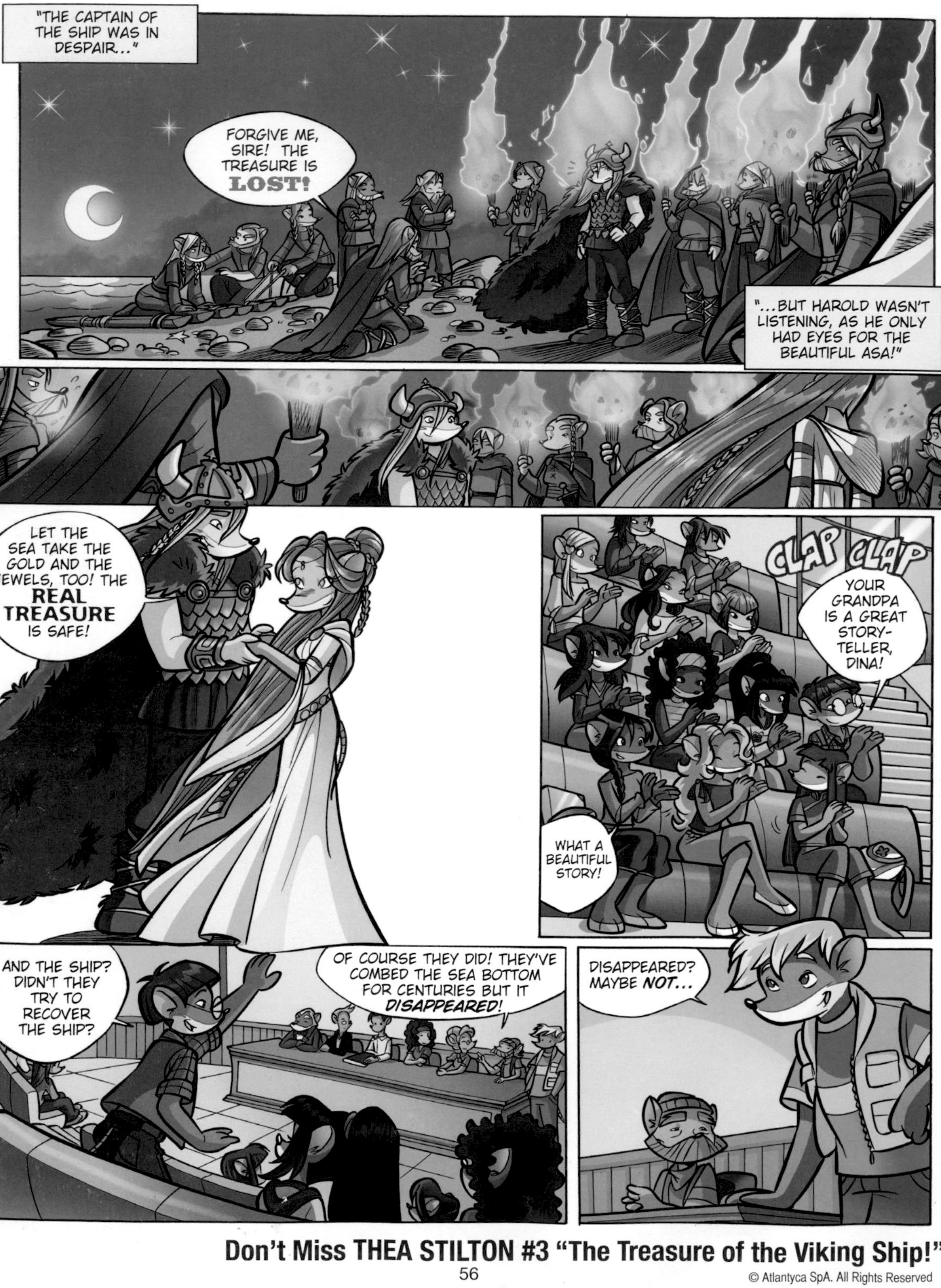
"THE CAPTAIN OF THE SHIP WAS IN DESPAIR..."
FORGIVE ME, SIRE! THE TREASURE IS LOST!
"...BUT HAROLD WASN'T LISTENING, AS HE ONLY HAD EYES FOR THE BEAUTIFUL ASA!"
LET THE SEA TAKE THE GOLD AND THE JEWELS, TOO! THE REAL TREASURE IS SAFE!
CLAP CLAP
YOUR GRANDPA IS A GREAT STORY-TELLER, DINA!
WHAT A BEAUTIFUL STORY!
AND THE SHIP? DIDN'T THEY TRY TO RECOVER THE SHIP?
OF COURSE THEY DID! THEY'VE COMBED THE SEA BOTTOM FOR CENTURIES BUT IT DISAPPEARED!
DISAPPEARED? MAYBE NOT...

Don't Miss THEA STILTON #3 "The Treasure of the Viking Ship!"

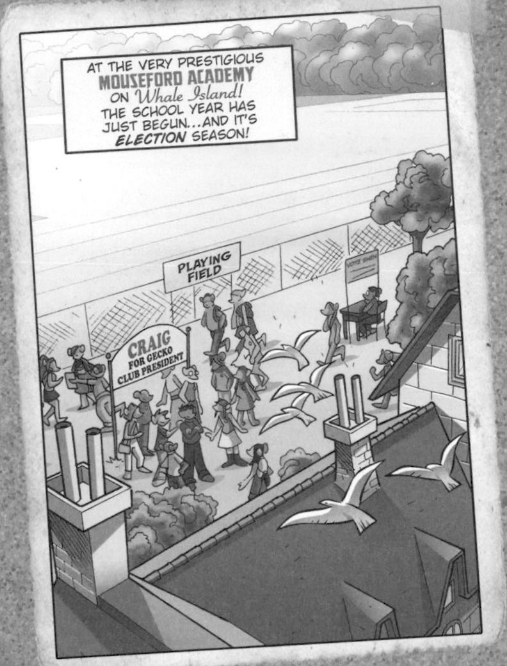
AT THE VERY PRESTIGIOUS MOUSEFORD ACADEMY ON Whale Island! THE SCHOOL YEAR HAS JUST BEGUN... AND IT'S ELECTION SEASON!
PLAYING FIELD
CRAIG FOR GECKO CLUB PRESIDENT

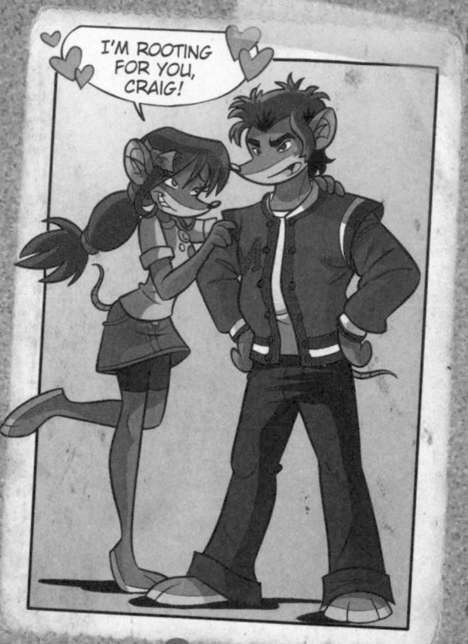
I'M ROOTING FOR YOU, CRAIG!

Craig is a Mouseford student, terrific at sports but not so good at his studies! He and Vic de Vissen compete for the hearts of the girls at the Academy.

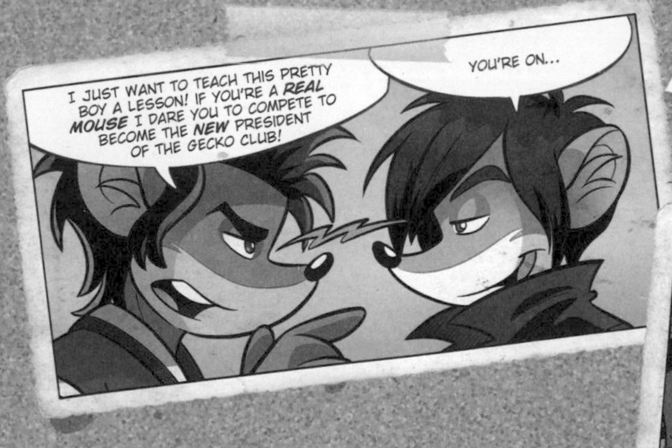
I JUST WANT TO TEACH THIS PRETTY BOY A LESSON! IF YOU'RE A REAL MOUSE I DARE YOU TO COMPETE TO BECOME THE NEW PRESIDENT OF THE GECKO CLUB!
YOU'RE ON...

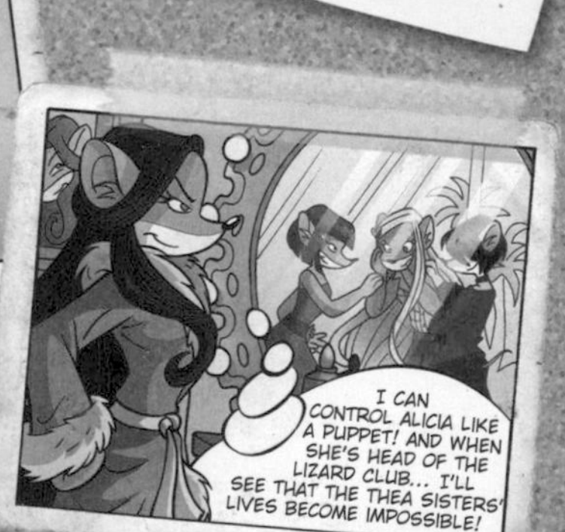
I CAN CONTROL ALICIA LIKE A PUPPET! AND WHEN SHE'S HEAD OF THE LIZARD CLUB... I'LL SEE THAT THE THEA SISTERS' LIVES BECOME IMPOSSIBLE!